Rd Read
D.C. 2024

S0-FAH-088

THE TEMPORARY AMISH NANNY

AMISH MISFITS BOOK 5

SAMANTHA PRICE

AMISH ROMANCE

Copyright © 2017 by Samantha Price

All rights reserved.

No part of this book may be reproduced in any form or by any electronic or mechanical means, including information storage and retrieval systems, without written permission from the author, except for the use of brief quotations in a book review.

This is a work of fiction. Any names or characters, businesses or places, events or incidents, are fictitious. Any resemblance to actual persons, living or dead, or actual events is purely coincidental.

CHAPTER 1

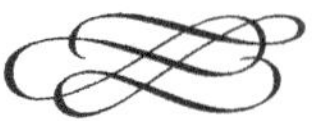

Deborah Fisher was pinning out the washing with Jenny, her younger sister, while she looked forward to a visit from their older sister, Elizabeth. Elizabeth had left the family home two years ago to marry Peter Yoder, and in a few months they were expecting their first child.

"I was just about to get that one," Jenny said with a giggle as they both reached for the same towel.

"You have to be quicker."

"What time did Elizabeth say she was coming?" Jenny asked, looking over her shoulder at the road in front of the house.

"She didn't really say a time. You know what she's like; she takes no notice of the hour of the day. She'll be here when she feels like it."

"I know. I wonder if she'll change when she's a *mudder.*"

"Maybe. She'll have to get the children to school on time."

"I can't wait until the *boppli's* born. I'll be an *aenti.*"

"So will I." Deborah wondered how long it would take her to become a mother. It would be good to have a niece or a nephew, but being a mother would be so much better. She longed for that day to come. Firstly, she'd have practice taking care of a newborn by helping her sister as much as she could. Secondly, she'd need a husband.

With Elizabeth now living with her new husband, things were a lot quieter in the family home, but their fourteen-year-old younger brother, Joshua, kept things interesting. He was always getting himself into some kind of trouble or other.

"I can't wait until you get married, too."

"I need someone to be interested in me first," Deborah said.

"I want to have a lot of nieces and nephews."

Deborah giggled as she reached for another towel in the basket by her feet. "I'll do my best, but I'm not … I might never marry. You might even marry before I do."

Jenny's jaw dropped open. "I'm only fifteen. No one marries at my age and I don't even like anyone."

"I didn't mean you'd get married now. What I meant was when you're eighteen or something you'll marry and I'll be still looking to find someone who appreciates me. I hope not, though."

"Your pimples have gone now if that's what you're worried about, and you don't even have any scars from them like some people do."

Deborah didn't need to be reminded about all the awful eruptions that had once covered her face. "That's something, I guess." She looked down at herself. "But I'm a lot bigger than other girls, if you haven't noticed."

"You'll get a man who loves you just as you are."

Deborah smiled at her sister's words. That was her hope. She desperately wanted to have someone to love and to care for, but how could she do that when no men came near her? How could they find out what her personality was like? She knew it was looks that attracted a man to a woman, and then it was her personality that kept him there. Her family loved her; surely, she'd find a man who loved her too.

She was eighteen already and had never been asked out on a date, never even gone on a buggy ride. That was due to her being a large girl, she knew that, and there was nothing she could do about it. Most of the time her size didn't bother her and she didn't want to lose weight just to attract a man. On the other hand, maybe she should if she wanted to marry. It was an ongoing mental struggle that plagued her daily. That one true special man, the one God had created just for her, would love her in any package she came in—wouldn't he?

Suddenly, a wet towel landed across her black lace-up boots. She looked up to see that Jenny had just dropped it.

"It's Elizabeth!" Jenny ran off to greet Elizabeth and Deborah was left to pick up the wet towel and pin out the last of the washing.

Sometimes Deborah felt like the mother. With their mother being the community midwife, she was often out of the house for several hours at a time. Their father worked long hours on the dairy farm he owned with his brother. Deborah was often left in charge of the everyday chores that kept the household running.

When Deborah finished with hanging out the washing, she picked up the basket, placed it on her hip, and walked toward her older sister.

Elizabeth was just securing the buggy while Jenny talked to her non-stop. Deborah's gaze immediately fell to Elizabeth's rounded belly.

"You're getting so big," Deborah said as soon as Jenny had stopped talking to take a breath.

Elizabeth finished securing the horse and touched her stomach with both hands. "I am, aren't I?" she said with a laugh. "I'm sure I've gotten bigger just in the last couple of days."

"You have. You're huge,"

"Is *Mamm* home?"

"Nee, she's not back yet. She's assisting at the birth of an *Englisch* woman who wanted to have a home birth."

"Let's go inside." Jenny grabbed Elizabeth's arm and started walking.

"Okay. Is there anything to eat? I'm starving."

Deborah followed the two of them into the house.

"We had pot roast last night and there's plenty left over. I could make you a toasted sandwich," Jenny said.

"Perfect."

Deborah placed the laundry basket into the laundry room and then sat down at the kitchen table with Elizabeth.

Elizabeth looked around. "Where's Joshua?"

"He's gone to work with *Dat* for work experience," Deborah said.

Elizabeth nodded. "That will do him good. Keeping him out of trouble. Anyway, I'm here to talk about you."

"Me?" Deborah asked.

"Jah, I found a job for you, if you're still looking for one."

"Really? Where?"

"Not far from here. Very close by, actually. It's looking after two children."

Deborah was thrilled. She loved children. "How old are they?"

"Two girls, six, and eight."

She took a wild guess. "You mean Nathan Beiler's *dochders?"* Nathan Beiler was a widower, but had been engaged to Elizabeth's best friend, Marta, going on two years.

"That's right. Marta has to go away to look after her *grossmammi* and she wants to make sure the girls are looked after. Nathan said she can find someone to fill in for her."

At first Deborah was delighted that Marta would put so much trust in her, but she could tell by her sister's face that there was more to this than she was letting on. "What's really going on? Marta has never particularly liked me. She's barely even said two words to me in her whole life."

Elizabeth noticeably gulped. "She's a little worried that Nathan has never set the date for their wedding. She wonders if he's truly committed to her."

Now the job offer made more sense to Deborah. "And she's worried that a prettier girl might turn his head, is that it? But if she replaces herself with someone ugly and fat like me, she can look after her *grossmammi* and have nothing to worry about?"

"Deborah! *Nee,* not at all."

There was no conviction in Elizabeth's voice and Deborah knew she'd guessed Marta's plan. "It sounds just like that to me, and I won't do it." She folded her arms across her chest and looked straight ahead.

"It will pay the same as any other full-time job."

She whipped her head back around to look at Elizabeth. "I'd be paid—money?"

"*Jah,* of course, silly."

That made a big difference to Deborah. She knew she'd need money to support herself just in case she never married. Joshua would inherit their father's share of the dairy farm, that was already set in stone. Elizabeth was already married to a wonderful man, and her younger sister was so sweet and beautiful there was no doubt in Deborah's mind that Jenny would be married by eighteen. The last thing Deborah wanted was to be poor and unmarried and to be forced to live with one of her siblings' families, tucked away in a dark back bedroom. No! She would save her money—squirrel it away so she could live with dignity in a home of her own. It didn't even matter if it was small, even a one bedroom cottage would do. She'd make a life for herself, be independent and be happy.

"What do you say?" Elizabeth asked.

"Well, I have been looking for a job and since I can't do anything in particular, that hasn't been easy. Is the job mine if I want it?"

"*Jah,* Nathan said that Marta can find someone to replace her for when she's gone. He trusts her completely to make a good choice."

"You told her that already," Jenny said as she joined them at the table.

Elizabeth frowned at Jenny. "Where's my toasted sandwich?"

"It's under the grill. I had to cut the meat and then make the sandwich. Don't be so impatient. Does Nathan pay Marta, his own fiancée?"

"That's a nosy question," Elizabeth said.

Deborah was glad Jenny had asked that question because she was wondering about that herself.

"If you must know, Nathan tries to make her take money for all the cooking and cleaning and looking after the children she does, but she won't take any money. She'd be doing it all if she was married to him, anyway."

"Why aren't they married by now, then?" Jenny asked.

"Just between us sitting here, that's what Marta's worried about. She's hoping that time away will make him miss her."

"So her *grossmammi* isn't really sick?" Jenny asked.

"Nee, Marta wouldn't be that conniving. She is really sick."

"Ah, I get it, and she's the only one in her whole extended and large family available to go and look after her."

Elizabeth shook her head at her younger sister and Deborah too could smell the plot a mile away. Whether Marta's grandmother was sick or not, Marta was trying to push Nathan into setting a date for the wedding. Secondly her plot was to free Nathan of any temptation or distraction caused by having a pretty woman under his nose every day. That's why she was chosen. It was clear that Marta was hoping Nathan would miss everything about her. "You told Marta I can cook and clean, didn't you?"

"I said all good things about you and that's why she's offered you the job."

"Are you sure it's all right with Nathan?"

"I'm positive."

"What kind of things would I have to do?"

"Nathan leaves for work early. You'd have to be there before he leaves, then cook the children breakfast, walk them to and from school. Then just do a bit of housework while they're away and then cook the evening meal. As soon as Nathan comes home you can leave."

Deborah slowly nodded. "It's good that he lives close by. I can even walk there. But I'll ride my bike and that'll be even quicker. When would I start?"

Elizabeth turned to Jenny. "Don't burn it."

"I'll get it out now." Jenny jumped up from the table.

"Tomorrow morning?"

"That soon?"

"I kind of told her that you'd do it. Only because I was sure you would. I know you love children, and you were looking for a job. Just make sure you're there early."

"Is Marta going to be there tomorrow to show me what to do?"

"She said she'd write out a long list and leave it for you. Nathan will be there when you get there. There's nothing to worry about."

Jenny placed the toasted sandwich in front of Elizabeth.

"Denke, Jenny, this looks *wunderbaar."*

Deborah watched Elizabeth bite into the sandwich as if she hadn't seen food for days. It was interesting to watch her sister turn into a mother. Now she'd know what to expect if her turn ever came.

She was nervous about the next day, but it sounded like the perfect job for her even though it was only temporary. Besides that, it would give her work experience to enable her to get the next job.

Deborah'd had a secret crush on Nathan from the time she was a young girl. She was a little upset when he married Sally, and from there she'd put him out of her mind. Not long after Sally had their second child, she developed a terminal illness and from the time she was diagnosed to the time she died was only six months. Grace wasn't even one at the time that Sally died.

Now Nathan and Marta had been dating going on two years. Marta said they were getting married, but no one knew when.

CHAPTER 2

Marta

Marta's grandmother wasn't really ill, no more than usual. Marta had exaggerated her grandmother's illness to get away from her life for a while. She had to clear her head and sort out her feelings for Nathan. She was desperately in love with him, but what good was that if he wasn't in love with her?

Two years was too long for an engagement. Something wasn't right. For the past year she'd been like the nanny and housekeeper. The fact that he was forcing her to take a weekly wage didn't sit well with her. She kept that quiet from her friends because they would think it odd that her fiancé was paying her. And why would he insist upon doing that? It was a way to put emotional distance between them, she thought. It made her feel like she was an employee rather than his intended wife.

Marta had sat on her grandmother's couch ever since she got there, crying as she told her grandmother about every aspect of her life. Now she was wrapped in a blanket with a mug of hot noodle soup in her hands.

"Do you see what I've been going through?" She hoped her grandmother would give her some good advice.

"I think you done the right thing in getting away. It'll give you a new view of things."

"I hope you're right. I miss Nathan and the children dreadfully."

"Perhaps he will miss you too, and come after you."

Marta shook her head. *"Nee,* he won't. I told him that you were sick and I have to come and look after you."

"Oh, I see. I hope word doesn't get around that I'm ill."

"I'm sorry, *Mammi.* I didn't think it through."

"No matter. Perhaps his hesitations have got something to do with Sally. He could see a second marriage as a betrayal."

"Do you think so? I didn't even think of that."

"It's possible. How long has it been since she died?"

"About five years."

"That's not a very long time. He was engaged to you three years after his wife died?"

"That's right. Now I'm worried that I forced him into it."

"How would you force it?"

She looked down at the noodles floating

on top of the soup, and then back into her grandmother's steely blue eyes. “I asked him to marry me. Do you see, he didn’t ask me? What if he was just saying yes to be polite?”

“He wouldn’t have said yes to be polite. He would’ve only said yes if he was in love with you. Has he told you he’s in love with you in so many words?”

“Nee, he hasn’t. Not even when I’ve told him I love him. The girls were excited that we were getting married when we first got engaged, but now they hardly even mention it. It was as though it never even happened. He’s forcing me to take money for helping out with the girls every day, and now I just don’t know what to do.”

“Try to think about something else for a while. Come to the quilting bee with me tomorrow.”

Marta sighed. “That’s the last thing I feel like doing. I don’t want to go out and face people and have them all ask questions. Do your friends know I’m engaged?”

"I'll tell them not to ask you any questions."

"Nee, that would be weird. Everything's just awkward and horrible."

"You can't just sit here wrapped in a blanket feeling sorry for yourself."

That's exactly what she wanted to do. How could she face the world when she'd told everyone she was going to marry Nathan, and now that didn't seem like it was going to happen? "Can't I stay here forever?"

"Not if I have anything to say about it. Tomorrow, it's the quilting bee. We're working on a quilt to auction at a special charity event. Instead of feeling sorry for yourself, you can concentrate on helping the less fortunate."

Seeing the grim look on her grandmother's face made her feel terrible. Her grandmother was trying to be understanding and sympathetic, but she knew *Mammi* really wanted to tell her to snap out of it. That's what her mother had said, and that was why she'd had to get away. There is no snapping out of it when you are losing the man you love. Why couldn't the older women in her family understand that? Not wanting to get on the wrong side of her grandmother and get herself sent right back home, she said, "The only sewing I've done lately is dresses for the girls."

"Put Nathan and his girls right out of your head. There's no point going over and over things. You're here for a rest from them, so have one."

"I just want him to miss me," she said in a small voice.

"He will miss you, don't you worry about that."

"Do you think so?"

Her grandmother grunted, but Marta couldn't stop thinking about the man she loved and had loved for two whole years. "I arranged for one of my friend's *schweschders* to fill in for me. I chose someone he wouldn't find attractive."

"That's silly! If his head could be turned so easily by another girl, he doesn't deserve you and isn't right for you."

Marta nodded, knowing her grandmother's words were true. "His head won't be turned by Deborah so there's nothing to worry about." She took a mouthful of the noodle soup and wondered why Nathan didn't find her good enough. Everyone else told her she was an attractive girl, and before Nathan, she'd had so many boys wanting to take her on buggy rides. Now most of those men had gotten married. Maybe she should've fallen in love with somebody who'd never been married before.

"What's on your mind now?" her grandmother asked.

"It's all so hard. Why is *Gott* testing me like this? Why couldn't He have given me a good man who loved me and had never been married before?" She fought back the tears and hoped her grandmother wouldn't rouse on her.

"Gott's ways are higher than our ways and that's why we can never figure out why He does what He does. All we can do is the best we can in every situation. You've done a smart thing by removing yourself and I'm glad you've come here to stay with me."

Marta shook her head. "It wasn't easy to leave. It wasn't easy at all. And you know what annoys me most?"

"What?"

"He's probably not even thinking about me or missing me."

"Well, that's your answer then. You'll have to stop working for him, stop seeing him and change your life. Make a new life without him. Perhaps move here with me. You can live here for awhile."

"Denke, Mammi. That's a kind offer, but I can't start over with someone new, with someone I don't know."

"There are nice men here, and one or two are the right age for you, and they have never been married. We also have two very nice widowers. If you don't settle for someone new, you're just setting yourself up for more disappointment. Break the pattern now, and the sooner, the better."

"You're talking as though he doesn't love me."

"Time will tell, and if you find out he doesn't want to marry you, you can't continue the way things have been. These are the best years to find a man and the longer you wait the less choice you'll have."

Marta slowly nodded while her stomach swam with frustration. She should've left several months ago. Hanging around waiting for Nathan to set a date had proved to be a complete waste of time. Then she thought about Emma and Grace. She so badly wanted to be their mother.

CHAPTER 3

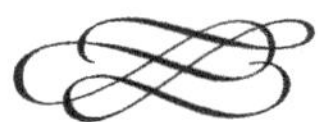

Deborah

When Deborah went to get her bike from the barn, she could see before she reached it there was something wrong with it. She grabbed the handlebars and pulled on them in an effort to move it out into the light. The wheels wouldn't even turn. She crouched down and saw that the frame on the wheel was badly twisted.

"Joshua!" she said through gritted teeth. He always had something wrong with his own bike and was always borrowing hers. It wasn't as though she minded, but he should have told her he'd damaged it, so she could've had it fixed.

Now she was going to be late on the first day of her new job. She glanced back at the house. If she took the family buggy, that would leave her mother and sister home with no transport and her mother needed to have a buggy at all times for her work as a midwife. Of course, her mother could drive her to Nathan's as well, but by the time the horse was hitched to the buggy, she'd still be late. Not only that, her mother had gotten home in the early hours of the morning after a late night delivering a baby. The only thing she could do was run, and that was something she hadn't done for a very long time.

She tied her prayer *kapp* strings under her chin so it wouldn't fly off, and then tied her boot laces into double knots. She set off down the driveway at a slow pace. If she ran flat out, she knew she'd tire before too long. After a few minutes of slow running, she got a sharp pain in her side. She changed her pace from slow running to brisk walking, hoping to ease the pain.

When the Beiler house came into view, she hoped she wasn't too late. She could lose her job before she even started.

The last dozen paces, she slowed right down so she wouldn't be puffing too much. She stepped onto the porch and saw Emma and Grace pressing their noses against the window. Deborah waved to them and they waved back and giggled.

The door suddenly opened and Nathan stood there with deep frown lines marring his forehead. He was as handsome as always with his rich chocolate-brown hair, honey-golden skin, and dark brown-almost-black eyes. "You're here at last. I was beginning to worry that you wouldn't show."

"I'm sorry, I was going to ride my bike, but then there was a problem with that – "

"Come inside." He stepped aside to allow her through.

"Marta said she gave you a list of what to do."

"*Nee.* I don't have it. I thought she was leaving it here. That's what she told my *schweschder.*"

He shook his head.

"I'm sorry, she hasn't given me a list."

"You've got nothing to be sorry for. Anyway, there's not much to know. You get the girls breakfast, walk them to school, and do what needs to be done around the place." He drew a deep breath. "Cook the evening meal, collect the girls from school. Apart from that, do the weekly shopping every Friday. On Fridays, you'll take me to work and then collect me. Does all that sound easy?" He grinned at her.

"*Jah,* I can manage all that." She looked around. "Where are the girls?"

"I sent them upstairs to get dressed for school."

"Have you already had breakfast?" Deborah remembered that was one of her duties.

"Jah, we have this morning."

"I'm so sorry I was late. It won't happen again. I'm usually so careful to be on time." She shook her head. "I should've checked the bike last night."

He grabbed his jacket and started to put it on. "What's wrong with it?"

"The wheel's twisted—the frame around the wheel to be exact."

"How did that happen? Did you have an accident?"

Deborah shook her head.

He smiled. "Joshua?"

"I'm guessing that's what happened to it. There's no other way it could've got that way. I certainly didn't do it and Joshua is the only other person in the family who rides bikes. Jenny won't ride one."

"Do you want me to take a look at it?"

"Ach nee, denke. I'm sure you're far too busy. I'll get my *vadder* to have a look at it."

"I'm not that busy."

"I won't be late in the future."

"Gut."

The girls ran down the stairs and ran toward Deborah who crouched down and gave them both a hug.

"Are you looking after us now?" Emma, the older girl, asked.

"That's right. For a little while at least."

"Are you gonna be marrying *Dat* now?" Grace asked.

Deborah laughed. *"Nee,* I'm not. Marta is still marrying your *vadder.* She'll just be gone for a few weeks." She looked over to see Nathan smiling.

Emma said, "Grace doesn't know much, she's only six."

"I know a lot," Grace said, pouting.

"I'm going now, girls." The girls hugged their father and then he headed to the barn to hitch his buggy.

"Now, you've cleaned your teeth and had

your breakfast?" The girls nodded. "We should go to school then."

"It's a little early," said Emma.

"It won't hurt us to be there a little early today."

Deborah walked out of the house still feeling unprepared for the day ahead. She hadn't even looked in the kitchen. There were probably dishes that needed washing, and then what would she cook for the evening meal? She didn't even know what kind of food they all liked.

"Where is Miss Marta?" Emma asked.

"She's gone to look after her sick *grossmammi.*"

"We need her here," Grace said.

"She'll be back. Don't worry."

The school was only a mile from the Beilers' house. When she was younger she and her sisters walked the three miles to school and three miles back home, right past the Beiler's house, which was two miles from hers. She wasn't overweight then, while she was still going to school. She hoped with all the extra walking she might lose a little weight, so she could be a little fitter and a little healthier.

When they reached the school gate, Emma turned around and looked at Deborah. "You won't be late collecting us, will you?"

"I'll be waiting right here for you." The girls each gave her a hug and she waited until they were inside the one-room schoolhouse.

As she walked back to Nathan's house, she was determined to do a good job. By the time she arrived, she was exhausted. It would've been a whole lot easier if she could've ridden her bike there this morning.

It was a typical thing for Joshua to wreck her bike and not tell her. She walked into the kitchen and saw that the washing up had not been done. Nathan wouldn't have had the time and he hadn't expected to have to cook the breakfast. She should've been there. She'd made a bad first-impression on her first day, and she wondered how she could make it up to Nathan. Perhaps she could cook him a very special meal, but what kind of food did he like? She had no idea.

Deborah looked around for any notes like what Marta had told Elizabeth she'd leave, but she hadn't left a thing. She did find a few recipe cards in the kitchen and the one that looked like it was most used was the one for spicy fried chicken. It made sense that the most worn recipe card would be for his favourite food, at least she hoped that was the case. She found some frozen chicken in the freezer section of the gas-powered fridge and took it out to thaw. Marta would've cooked good meals for the man she planned to marry, and for his two girls, and she couldn't put in less than the same effort. If she did a good job she would ask Nathan for a recommendation for a job when Marta returned.

All Deborah wanted to do was rest after so much walking, but she couldn't. There was so much to do. She drank a large glass of water and then washed up the breakfast dishes, all the while wondering why Nathan had never set a date for the wedding with Marta. Perhaps he was still too upset over his late wife to make that final commitment to another woman.

CHAPTER 4

Once the kitchen was clean, Deborah turned her attention to what else might need doing around the house. Things would've been so much easier if Marta had left her that list as she'd said. Nathan had told her to do whatever needed doing, but that was pretty wide open. The clothes hamper was empty, so she didn't need to wash any clothes. She set about sweeping the floors and dusting until it was time for lunch. Nathan had told her to help herself to anything that was in the fridge. In future, she would bring her own sandwich because she didn't like eating other people's food.

She made herself a peanut butter and jelly sandwich and sat down at the kitchen table to eat it. Her legs were still tingling from the running she'd done earlier that morning, so she stretched them out on the chair next to her.

When her break was over, she set about chopping some vegetables to save time later in the day. When the girls came home from school she hoped she'd have time to play with them rather than be stuck in the kitchen until their father came home.

She was rinsing out her lunch plate in the kitchen sink when she looked out the window and noticed a buggy coming to the house. A young Amish man was driving the buggy. When she looked harder, she realised it was Nathan's younger brother, Adam. She wiped her hands, and then stepped through the back door and walked out to meet him.

Adam looked up as he stepped down from the buggy. "Marta, you've changed."

Deborah giggled. "Marta's gone to look after her sick *grossmammi.* I'm not sure where she lives—somewhere far away."

"No one tells me anything around here. So, you're the new Marta?"

"I'm looking after the children while she's gone."

"And, looking after my *bruder,* it seems."

Deborah scrunched her shoulders. "I'm just doing what I need to do."

His lips turned downward at the corners and he shuddered. "Sounds boring."

She wondered why he was there. Surely, he'd know his brother would've already left for work. Or, had he come to see Marta? "Are you looking for your *bruder?"*

"Not particularly. I was visiting Marta."

Deborah nodded; she was right. Funny that he'd visit his brother's fiancée while Nathan was at work. "I heard you'd gone on *rumspringa."*

"I did, and now I'm back."

He was much more attractive than Deborah remembered him. He'd been gone a good six months and before that she'd never paid too much attention, preferring to focus all her secret attention on his older brother. "Where are you working now, Adam?"

"I'm looking for work."

"What do you do again?"

"A bit of this and a bit of that. Whatever I can find."

"It should be easy for you to find a job somewhere, then."

He tipped his hat back slightly on his head. "I'm hoping so. How long has Marta been gone?"

"Today is the very first day." Since he was here, she decided to make use of his visit. "Do you happen to know what Nathan's favorite food is?"

He tipped his head to the side. "Why?"

She laughed. "I'm hoping to cook a nice meal for him tonight. It's my first day, as I said, and I was late this morning and I feel dreadful about that. I thought if I made a *gut* meal, I might be able to redeem myself slightly."

"You should ask me what my favorite food is since I'm staying for dinner."

"Are you?"

He nodded.

"I got some chicken out of the freezer, but I'm just deciding what to do with it. And, I found a recipe card for spicy fried chicken. I'm hoping that's one of his favored dishes."

"Don't stress. My *bruder* and I have the same tastes in food. We like anything and we eat everything put before us. He'll like the one you mentioned, the spicy one."

"That's good to know." Nerves kept her talking. "Marta was going to leave me a list, so I'd know exactly what to do, but she didn't. I'm worried that I'm not going to do everything correctly."

"Relax. As long as someone's here for the *kinner* and to do a bit of this and a bit of that,

that's all that matters." He flashed her a smile and folded his arms across his chest.

From his words Deborah drew the conclusion that he was a careless kind of person. The "near enough is good enough" type. Although, he did seem kind, and he was being nice to her. Should she ask him inside? He was standing there talking, but she couldn't stand there all day. She had work to do. "Are you staying back at your *mudders' haus?"*

"I am, until I find a place of my own. I'm too old to live with my *mudder.* I'll have to, though, until I get some money behind me."

Deborah figured he would be about four years older than herself and that would make him around twenty-two. By her standards, he wasn't too old to still live at home. "I guess I should keep doing some work. Do you want to come inside? I can make you some *kaffe,* or something," Deborah said, nodding her head back toward the house.

"I could drive you to pick up the girls when it's time."

That was the best news Deborah had heard in ages. "Would you?"

"Jah. I figured we need to pick them up in an hour."

"That sounds about right."

"Are you going to ask me into the *haus?"*

She giggled. "I just did."

He chuckled. "I didn't hear. Can you make me a cup of *kaffe?"*

"Of course."

As they walked inside, he said, "Marta makes the best coffee."

"I'll try to make you a nice cup. How do you have it?"

"Just black with no sugar."

She pulled a face and he grinned at it. "Sounds a little nasty," she said.

"Some people think it is, but that's the way I've gotten used to it."

CHAPTER 5

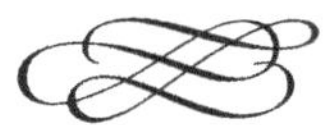

When they reached the kitchen, Adam sat at the kitchen table and watched Deborah make the coffee.

"Are you going to have one with me?"

"I guess I can take another break. I've only just had lunch, just a quick one."

"I'm sure my *bruder* won't mind you having a cup of *kaffe* with me."

"I won't have it without milk, though."

"Suit yourself."

She passed him his black coffee. "I hope that measures up to your standards."

He lifted it closer, looked at it, sniffed it and then took a sip. "Every bit as good as Marta makes."

"That's good. I'm nervous that I won't live up to Marta's standards."

"You don't have to. You're not Marta, you're yourself."

She grimaced. *"Denke* for reminding me. Sometimes, I'd rather be anybody else. *Mostly,* I'd rather be anybody else."

He stared at her with his dark brown eyes. "You should never wish to be like anybody else. Everyone is an individual and has both good points and bad points. You're unique and there's nobody like you in the whole world."

She giggled. "Is that what you learned on your *rumspringa?"*

His eyes twinkled and he wagged his finger at her. "I learned a lot, don't you worry about that."

"Are you back to stay, or do you think

you might leave again? Oh, sorry, I hope you don't mind me asking."

"I don't mind at all. I'm back to stay. I always intended to come back and I did. It's interesting to see what's out there in the world, but it can be a crazy place sometimes." He shook his head.

"I don't even want to go to see what it's like."

"Is this what you want to do with your life, look after other people's children?"

The question caught her by surprise. "I've only been here a day-not even that."

"Well? What if you have to do this for two more years like Marta's done."

"I want to get married someday when I'm older, and have a couple of children, not too many. I don't want to have more than six. I think I'd like to have four, but certainly not any more than that. And if I don't marry, I will live in a small white cottage on the riverfront with two dogs."

He laughed. "That's a lot of information."

"Well, you asked."

"Yeah, I did."

She took a sip of coffee. "Anyway, what about yourself?"

"I guess I'll get married at some time. When I can talk the right woman into it."

"And?" She leaned forward.

"And what?"

"Oh, come on! I told you a lot more than that."

He chuckled. "A small *familye* is fine for me too, but first I'm gonna need a *fraa."*

"That always helps, I suppose."

"And before that a job is sorely needed. It's the first thing I need to get."

"Can't Nathan give you a job at his furniture store? I heard he's opening another one soon."

He immediately grinned and sipped his hot *kaffe,* keeping silent.

Deborah nodded. "Ah, that's why you've come here for dinner?"

"That's right. I thought I'd slip it into the

conversation that I'm looking for a job, and then see what he says." He chuckled.

"You couldn't just ask him?"

"I couldn't do that, because then he would think he was doing me a favor. I wanted to be more businesslike than that. I don't want him giving me a job just because I'm his *bruder.*"

"Wouldn't that be a good reason to give you a job—the best reason?"

He took another sip. "You don't understand."

She guessed from his answer that the two brothers hadn't always gotten along. "Probably not. Do you know anything about furniture?"

"Enough to sell it."

"So, you're going to hope he gives you a job selling the furniture?"

"Jah, selling. I can sell things. I've had sales jobs before. I can't make furniture. I can't saw in a straight line. Nathan was always good at woodwork, just like our

vadder was. That's why he was the favored son."

"I'm sure that's not true."

He slowly nodded looking into his drink. "It was true. My *mudder* loves us equally, but my *vadder* made no secret of preferring Nathan."

He looked so sad that Deborah wanted to change the subject. "What did you sell in your other jobs?"

"I had a job for a time selling tires."

"Tires for cars?"

"Jah."

"Did you work anywhere else?"

"I worked at a fast food place. Are you giving me an interview or something, Deborah? Do you have a job for me?"

Deborah laughed. "If I were giving you an interview, I would point out that you're not really selling when you work at a fast food place, you're taking people's orders. They already know what they want when they come in."

"For your information, there's something called add-on-sales."

"Do you mean when they say, *do you want fries with that?*"

Adam laughed. "I see your point. I guess I was trying to stretch things too far."

"Just a little bit."

He stared at her and she got embarrassed and looked away. When she looked back, he was still staring at her.

"What?" she asked.

"You've changed from how you used to be."

"And how was that?"

"You were quiet and never said boo. Now you've got an opinion about everything."

"That's a good thing, isn't it?"

"You're different from a lot of other girls in the community."

She wondered if he was flirting with her. Having never been flirted with made it hard to tell, but he was certainly making her feel good about herself. Glancing at the clock on the wall, she said, "It's nearly time for us to leave for the girls."

"Gut. I'm looking forward to seeing them."

"I'm sure they'll be pleased to see you too. Have you seen them since you've been gone? Did you call on them while you were on *rumspringa?"*

"I didn't and I feel bad about that now. I should've. They would've grown up so much. And I've missed both their birthdays. That's why I brought them both presents."

Deborah laughed. "Then they'll be doubly pleased to see you."

He nodded. "I want to be their favorite *onkel."*

"Aren't you their only *onkel?"*

"Sally had two brothers."

"Oh, I didn't know. Do Emma and Grace see much of them?"

"Nee, they both live in Ohio."

"Then you have the advantage over them."

He smiled.

Deborah looked at the uncut vegetables. When the girls got home they would be playing with their uncle and then she would have time to cook the dinner.

"Did you say this is your first job?" he asked.

"I don't remember if I said it, but it is. First day at my first job."

"And how do you like it so far?"

"I'm sure I'll love it."

He looked around the kitchen and his eyes rested on the vegetables at the other end of the table. "It's a pretty easy kind of a job."

"Have you ever cooked, cleaned, washed and looked after children?"

"Nee, but it can't be too hard. You're not out in the hot sun hammering on a roof, or doing all sorts of other heavy outside work."

"It can still be high pressure and full of tension. But I guess it beats outside heavy physical work."

"I finally found something you agree with me on."

"I haven't been disagreeing with you, just discussing."

He smiled at her and then drained the last of his coffee. "I'm ready when you are." He placed the mug back on the kitchen table.

"Okay, I'm ready."

CHAPTER 6

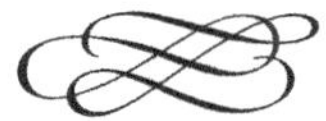

They were both silent as the buggy clip-clopped its way through the tree-lined streets on the way to the girls' school. It made Deborah feel very grown-up to be riding in a buggy with a handsome man. She imagined for a moment that she was married to Adam and they were collecting their own girls from school. It gave her a sense of peace and satisfaction. That made her wonder whether Adam might be a good match for her. He didn't have a job, but he was handsome and he had plans for the future. She knew he came from a good family and his parents had always gotten along well with hers.

When they arrived at the school, he stopped the buggy behind two others.

"I should get outside, so they'll see I'm here. They're not expecting to be collected in a buggy."

"Okay, but stay here until we see children start to come out. I can't believe that he makes you walk all that way to and from school. My father used to take us to school in the wagon. Nathan never had to walk."

"It doesn't hurt them. Or me. It's only a mile. It's good exercise. We had a lovely talk on the way this morning. And it's not far if they're used to it."

Adam shook his head. "I don't like it. Until I get a job, I'll take them to and from school."

Deborah was delighted that she wouldn't have to walk the distance.

"What do you think about that?" he asked, staring at her.

"It sounds like a good idea as long as you don't mind doing it."

"It's fine. It's not as though I'm doing anything else except looking for a job. And I can do that at other times of the day unless I have a job interview. I'll talk to Nathan about it tonight."

Deborah looked over at the schoolhouse. "They're coming out now." She jumped out of the buggy and waited with a group of parents.

"Hello, Deborah."

Deborah looked around to see Maggie Miller, the local gossip. "Hello, Maggie."

"Why are you here?"

"I'm looking after Nathan Beiler's children while Marta is looking after her sick *grossmammi.*"

Maggie turned and looked back at Adam's buggy. "Adam's back."

Deborah noticed Adam was out of the buggy and walking toward them.

"That's right. He just got back from *rumspringa.*"

She raised her eyebrows. "Nice of him to drive you here."

"*Jah,* it was."

They were interrupted by Grace's squeal as she ran out from the schoolroom toward Adam, who was now standing behind her and Maggie. The teacher walked out after the children, asking Grace to be quiet. Emma followed close behind her sister and they both hugged Adam and asked him if he was going to stay.

Deborah felt everyone was staring at them and she hoped the teacher wasn't going to mention Grace's squeals to her father. She recalled her own schooldays where they'd had to walk out of the schoolroom in single file, and they were not allowed to make any noise until they reached the road and were off the school grounds.

Adam scooped Grace into his arms and held onto Emma's hand as they walked back to his buggy.

Emma turned around to look at Deborah, then ran to her and gave her a quick hug. "I didn't see you."

Deborah laughed. "I saw you."

"Hello, Miss Deborah." Grace said, looking back while she was being carried.

"Hello."

Emma hurried back to take hold of her uncle's hand. Deborah could see how good Adam was with children by the affection his nieces had for him.

While they traveled back to the house, the girls were pleased to hear that their uncle was staying close by and not leaving again.

"Are you going to keep looking after us every day, Miss Deborah, now that *Onkel* Adam is back?"

"I am, because *Onkel* Adam will be looking for a job."

Emma scrunched her face. "Why are you

calling him *Onkel* Adam? He's not your *onkel.*"

"That's true. Very true, Emma. I was calling him that because he's your *Onkel* Adam."

"That doesn't make sense," Emma said.

"I suppose it doesn't. I'll just call him Adam from now on."

"Okay."

CHAPTER 7

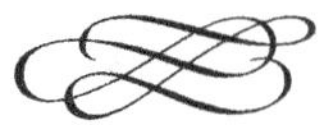

When they got home, the girls played with Adam while Deborah worked on the evening meal. She was having a much better time than if she'd stayed at home.

It seemed odd to cook the meal and then leave without eating it, and she wondered whether that's what Marta had done. She guessed she would have cooked and then gone home as soon as Nathan got home. That would make more sense. Otherwise she would have been going home too late and in the dark.

The girls ran into the kitchen and requested a lot of mashed potatoes, telling her they ate that every night and their father liked them as well. They confirmed that their father liked the spicy fried chicken.

When she saw Nathan's buggy coming toward the house, she let the others know. The girls ran out to meet him and Adam followed along behind. It was obvious Nathan wasn't expecting him because of the look of amazement on Nathan's face. Then she had a horrible thought. What if she was supposed to bathe the girls before dinner? It had totally slipped her mind. She walked to the front to meet Nathan when he came in the front door.

He walked through the door with a girl holding each hand and Adam behind him.

"I hear you've been entertaining this stranger, Deborah," Nathan said.

"Jah, I hope that's okay." Deborah chuckled. "I barely recognized him."

"Me either. He's certainly changed."

"I haven't even been gone a year. I couldn't have changed that much."

The girls quickly asked Adam to go to their room with them because they had something to show him. When he left the room, Deborah had a chance to talk with Nathan.

"I'm not sure of the routine yet. Should I have bathed the girls before now?"

"Jah, they're generally bathed and ready for bed when I get home. The girls do chores every afternoon, too. I'm guessing they haven't done any today with the excitement of Adam being here?"

"That's right. They haven't done any chores." Deborah felt like she was failing badly. She shouldn't have given so much attention to the evening meal. "Do you know what chores Marta had them do?"

"All I know is that when I came home, dinner was ready, the girls were washed and ready for bed, and the place was neat and tidy, and clean." He looked around his house. "I can see you've been keeping busy."

Deborah was relieved that he seemed pleased with the amount of housework she'd done.

"And dinner smells amazing," he added.

"It's fried chicken and there's plenty of mashed potatoes because the girls tell me that you all like them."

He chuckled. "We do. We all love potatoes."

"Shall I give the girls a bath and then go, or shall I serve the dinner and then go? The table's all set and ready."

"*Jah,* please get the girls bathed and then you can stay for dinner if you wish since my *bruder's* here."

"Oh, *nee,* that's okay. I don't want to be in the way."

Adam walked into the room with the girls close behind him. "You won't be in the way."

"It's just that I didn't tell my *mudder* I would be having dinner here. She'll be expecting me home." Deborah didn't really know what her mother was expecting because she'd told her nothing, but Deborah was too nervous to stay longer.

"That's understandable."

"I can drive you home when you're ready to go," Adam said.

Deborah turned around and saw the two girls, one hanging onto each of Adam's hands. "*Nee,* that's alright. It's not far and the dinner is nearly ready."

"I'm sure dinner will wait. It won't take me long to drive you and get back."

With her legs still aching, she appreciated him being insistent and took him up on the offer. "Okay *denke*. I'll just give the girls a bath first."

After she had bathed the girls, she helped them dress ready for bed.

"What kind of chores did Miss Marta give you when you got home from school?" she asked the girls when she finished dressing them.

"Sometimes we do gardening," Emma said.

"Sometimes we folded clothes after Marta washed them."

"You mean after they were dry," Emma corrected her younger sister.

"*Jah,* when they were dry we folded them. She told us how to fold everything properly."

Deborah wondered whether Emma still remembered their mother. She would've been only three when Sally died but she might have faint memories, whereas Grace would've been far too young.

"Can we come with you for the ride when Adam takes you home?" Emma asked.

"Not now that you're dressed for bed. It's

best that you wait here and Adam won't be very long. I don't live very far away."

"We know where you live," Emma said. "We've been there before."

"Jah, I know you have." Deborah's house often had the fortnightly Sunday meetings held there. Her parents' house was large, and they also had a large open area between the barn and the house which was perfect for the summer open-air meetings.

Deborah took the girls back downstairs. After a quick look in the kitchen to ensure that everything was cooked properly, she was satisfied with the first day's work.

Nathan came up behind her. "*Denke* for today, Deborah. I appreciate you being able to do this at short notice."

"I enjoyed it. Your girls are lovely."

He chuckled. *"Jah,* I think so."

"I hope Marta's *grossmammi* will be okay."

"Jah, we all do. I'm sure she'll be fine."

Deborah was surprised to hear him say that. Either he had a lot of faith in God, or he suspected that Marta was plotting. "Are you shocked Adam came back so soon?"

"I heard he was coming back. Although, I didn't expect to see him here today."

Deborah turned her attention back to the food. "I hope it's not ruined. The mashed potatoes were made a while ago and kept heated." She pulled a face knowing they were better mashed just before serving. "I hope they haven't dried out. I should've mashed them just before I left. I'm sorry. The chicken should be okay—I hope."

"It smells delicious. I'm sure everything will be perfect. Even if it's not, it would be far better than I can cook."

"Are you ready?" Adam asked as he walked into the kitchen.

"Jah, I'm ready." She turned to Nathan. "I'll be on time tomorrow, I'll make sure of it."

He chuckled. "Let me know if you'd like me to take a look at your bike. It's no trouble."

"Denke, Nathan. I'll let you know if my *vadder* can't fix it." She said goodbye to the girls and walked out of the house with Adam. *"Denke* for driving me home. It's very nice of you. I'm not used to doing so much walking. I've done a fair bit today." They both climbed into the buggy.

"I don't like walking either. If I'm going to go somewhere on foot I'd rather run so I get there faster."

"That sounds like it could be quite exhausting."

He moved his horse forward. "It is, that's why we've got horses and buggies."

Deborah chuckled. "I guess so."

In no time, her house came into sight.

"Here we are already," he said slowing his horse.

"I hope your *bruder* offers you a job."

"Denke, so do I."

"I'm sure he will if he has a vacancy."

"If he doesn't, something else will turn up."

Just as he was moving onto the driveway, she said, "Don't bother about taking me up to the front door, just let me out here."

"Are you sure? It's no bother to take you all the way."

Seeing she'd have a lot of explaining to do if anyone saw Adam Beiler, she insisted, "That's fine. Just let me out here."

"As you wish." He brought the buggy to a halt.

"*Denke,* Adam. I guess I'll see you at the meetings, or something."

"I said I'd drive you and the girls to school tomorrow. So, I'll see you at Nathan's *haus* in the morning." He turned the horse and was gone before she could say anything about that.

As Deborah walked to the house, her legs felt like lead weights. She knew with more walking, she'd get used to it and then she'd be fine.

When she walked into the house, she smelled the dinner and was pleased to see that it was on the table. Everybody was waiting for her, to find out how her first day went.

"Did you do a good job?" Joshua asked.

"I think so. I think Nathan was pleased with what I did today. I could have done better if only I had known what the routine was. Marta said she was going to leave me a list of instructions, but there was nothing at Nathan's *haus.*"

"I think I would like a job looking after kids," Jenny said.

Their father chuckled. "You're just a kid yourself."

"I am not. I'm grown-up, *Dat.*"

Mamm said, "You might think you're grown up but you're not yet, not really. When you're eighteen like Deborah, then you'll be grown up."

"I don't see the difference. There is no difference between me and Deborah."

"You're immature, Jenny," Joshua said which made everybody giggle.

"Do you even know what that means?" Deborah asked her brother.

"Of course, I do. That's when someone is supposed to be a certain age and they act a lot younger."

Jenny pouted, clearly not liking her younger brother's description of her.

"Now that you brought up being immature, Joshua, there's a little matter of my twisted bike wheel. I wasn't going to say anything."

"I'm sorry. I meant to tell you."

"What's this about?" *Dat* asked.

"I twisted the wheel of her bike. I borrowed it without asking and now I suppose I'm gonna get punished—stay in my room for six weeks." He stared at his father. "Shall I go there now?"

"You should, for been cheeky just now if for nothing else," *Mamm* said.

Deborah said, "It was just annoying because I was going to ride it to Nathan's this morning, and then I was late and I had to run nearly all the way there."

"Oh, how terrible, you had to run." Joshua rolled his eyes.

"Joshua and I will have a look at it tonight for you, Deborah. We'll try to have it fixed by morning."

Knowing how hard her father worked and how tired he must be, she said, "That's okay, *Dat*. I don't mind walking. It's just that I didn't leave enough time for that this morning and that's why I was late. I can walk tomorrow, it's fine. Don't do it tonight. I'd be pleased if you could both have a look at it on the weekend."

Her father nodded. "Very well."

Joshua looked at his father and then looked at his mother. "What's my punishment this time?"

"Give me some time to think about it," *Dat* said.

Joshua stuck a fork into his bologna. "I knew I wouldn't get away with it."

“Why should you get away with it. That’s immature. You’re immature, and not me!” Jenny said.

Deborah felt a little bad for mentioning the bike in front of their parents, but if she didn’t tell her father, who would’ve fixed it?

At the end of the meal, Deborah asked, "Can I get out of doing the washing up tonight? I’m exhausted, and I just want to go straight to bed.”

“You go right ahead. Now that you’ve got a full-time job, we can’t expect you to do work when you get home as well.”

Deborah liked the sound of her mother’s words. As soon as dinner was over, she showered and got ready for bed with barely enough energy left to change into her night-gown. When she finally got between the sheets, she closed her eyes and thought about her day. It had been strange to be in Nathan’s house. Years ago, when she’d had a crush on him, she would’ve loved to be in his house looking after his children. Back then, she’d been so young and then he'd married Sally. Now that she was older and now that he was a widower, he was still unattainable because he was in love with Marta. She tried to not let it bother her that pretty women like Marta had their choice of all the available men.

CHAPTER 8

Marta

Marta was sitting on the couch at her grandmother's house, still feeling sorry for herself. She'd managed to get out of going to the quilting bee, but she knew she had to leave the house sooner or later. When Marta heard her grandmother's phone ringing from the shanty directly outside the house, she ran to answer it hoping it was Nathan.

She tried not to sound breathless, as

though she'd run for the phone. Neither did she want to sound excited. "Hello." She was pleased with how she'd sounded, sweet and calm.

"Marta, it's me."

It wasn't Nathan, but it was a voice she knew. "Adam? Is that you?"

"Jah."

"Where are you?"

"I'm back from *rumspringa* and then I found out you'd gone. I was heartbroken."

Marta was pleased that at least she'd been missed by someone. "My *grossmammi* isn't very well. I had to take care of her. How's Nathan?"

"Just the same. I had dinner with him and the girls."

"How are they all?"

"Doing really well. You've only been gone a day, haven't you?"

"It seems like forever. How's my substitute working out?"

"Deborah?"

"*Jah,* she's still there, isn't she?"

"She is, and she's doing fine. She cooked a wonderful meal for us."

"Does that mean you and Nathan have made amends?"

"Not totally. That won't happen until you choose one or the other."

Marta giggled. "I've already made my choice, you know that. Don't make things even more difficult."

"In my book, you haven't made your choice until you're married. And you're not married now. What I want to know is, why not? Every day I was on *rumspringa* I expected a call telling me to come back for your wedding. I got no call and I returned to find out you're not even married. I should've continued trying to get you back. It was a silly choice to leave the community."

"I hope you didn't leave on account of me."

"It doesn't matter now. I'm back and I'm back to stay."

"I'm glad to hear it."

"Why don't I come there and see you? I've got a friend who lives around there somewhere, not far from your *grossmammi."*

"Nee, that would be the very worst thing you could do. Nathan would get the wrong idea."

"Why haven't you married him yet?"

"I'm waiting for him to organize a date for the wedding."

"You're waiting for him?"

"That's right." Marta hated to admit it. It was an awful feeling not knowing if Nathan truly wanted her or not. He had said he did, but that was so long ago. Why couldn't he be more like Adam?

"How long are you going to wait for him to set the date?"

The words were like a knife through her heart. She couldn't give him an answer.

"Marta? Are you still there?"

"I'm still here."

"You haven't answered my question."

"I don't have an answer." Marta had liked both Adam and Nathan, but had chosen Nathan because he was a better choice for a husband since he was older and more mature. Nathan also had his own successful business while Adam was nothing but a dreamer and a drifter. The last couple of years had proved her opinion of Adam right. He still had no direction in life. She needed stability and that was one of the many things she'd found so attractive about Nathan. "Adam, I have to go."

"No wait! Don't hang up."

"I'm sorry." She hung up the phone. It was too painful to speak to him. Standing there staring straight ahead, she noticed how cold the chilly night air was as it bit into her cheeks. Turning her face up to the starry night sky, she prayed to God for Him to guide her way. She wanted to be married and have a family, but now she knew she might have to let go of the idea of marrying Nathan for her dreams to come true.

For two years, she'd thought about nothing but a life and a future with Nathan and his two girls, but he wouldn't be pinned down about a date for the wedding. In the end, he refused to talk about it at all. She'd said nothing for months, hoping that with no pressure he'd eventually come around and set a date.

The whole thing was shameful. Everyone knew they were intended for one another, as good as engaged, so how would she explain things to people if they broke up? What would the two girls, Emma and Grace, think? They were looking forward to her being their mother.

She went to head back when she heard her grandmother opened the front door.

"I'm coming, *Mammi.*"

"You're certainly taking a long time. Come inside, it's cold out there."

"I'll be there in a minute, *Mammi.* I just want to give Elizabeth a quick call."

"Well, don't be long, or I'll be looking after *you* because you'll get a nasty cold."

"Okay. I won't be long." She waited until her grandmother was inside the house and made her call.

When she had finished asking Elizabeth a huge favor, Marta walked into the warm house, bitterly disappointed that the earlier phone call hadn't been from Nathan. She'd never felt so low.

CHAPTER 9

Deborah

The next morning, Deborah was shaken awake by Elizabeth. Fearing she was late for work Deborah sat upright. "Am I late?"

"*Nee.* You've got plenty of time. It's still early."

Deborah rubbed her eyes. "What time is it?"

"It's only six thirty."

She stared at her sister who was looking bright-eyed. "What are you doing here?"

"Marta called me last night and gave me some questions she wants you to ask Nathan."

"Oh good. You've got the list. I couldn't find it anywhere. I wonder why she gave it to you."

"This is nothing about the job there. This is personal. These are personal questions she wants you to ask him."

"I don't understand." Deborah yawned and wanted nothing more than to go back to sleep.

"It's simple. She wants you to find out some things from him."

"Such as?" Deborah didn't want to get involved with anything personal. She was only there to do a job.

"She wants to get to the bottom of how he feels about her. She doesn't want to waste her time with him."

Deborah felt sick to the stomach. "I can't

ask him anything like that."

"Of course not, but you can ask him things around and about the point without actually asking him."

Deborah brought her knees up to hug them. "I'm grateful that Marta recommended me for the job, but I'm not comfortable with what she's asking me to do."

Her sister licked her lips. "I quite understand, but put yourself in Marta's place. She's so upset. I could hear in her voice last night that she was close to tears. If we don't help her, who will?"

Deborah shook her head.

"Oh, come on! You've got to help her with this. She just needs to know if he's ever going to marry her."

"What makes you think that he'll tell me?"

"Just try."

Marta and Elizabeth were expecting far too much of her. "Surely it's between the two of them."

"Sometimes I think you're smart, and other times I think you're just selfish."

Deborah had never been called selfish before, and she didn't like it.

Her sister continued, "Put yourself in her situation. You're in love with a man, and it's been going on two years, and he won't commit."

"But he has committed, because he's said he'd marry her." She stared at Elizabeth. "Didn't he? They are engaged, aren't they?"

"What's the good of being engaged forever if the wedding date is never set? Who wants to be endlessly engaged? It's being married that counts. Marta doesn't want to wait forever. Wouldn't you want someone to help you if you were Marta?"

Deborah sighed. "I guess so. What are the questions?"

Elizabeth gave a little smile as she unfolded the paper in her hands.

Deborah was grateful that Elizabeth

drove her to Nathan's house on the way back to her home. It saved a long walk, and her father wasn't planning to look at her bike until the weekend.

CHAPTER 10

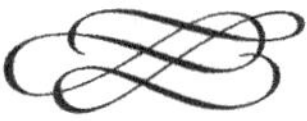

Deborah said goodbye to Elizabeth and headed up the drive to Nathan's house, pleased she was on time and would be there to cook breakfast for him and the girls. She could see Marta's point of view and why she was so distraught. If she'd been caring for Nathan and his girls for two years and there was no marriage on the horizon, it would've been just awful. Elizabeth was right, what good was an engagement without the wedding and the marriage that should follow?

She'd had Elizabeth let her out at the bottom of the driveway and she walked up to the house.

When she reached the door, she heard running footsteps and the girls got to the door first. They opened the door and both ran to her with open arms. She crouched down and hugged them and when she stood, Nathan was in front of her.

"Gut mayrie," he said. "You're a little earlier today."

"I know. I feel terrible about yesterday."

"Girls, let Miss Deborah get in the door."

The girls stepped away from her, and Grace said, "Are you taking us to school again today?"

"She's doing that every day. I told you that," Emma said to her younger sister.

"That's right," Deborah said. "Now, I'll make your breakfast, shall I?"

"Can we help?" Emma asked.

"Okay."

The girls took a hand each as they walked into the kitchen.

Deborah swung around and said to Nathan, "Would you like anything in particular for breakfast today?"

"Jah, kaffe, and bacon and eggs on toast."

Deborah nodded and then as she continued to the kitchen, Emma said, "We only like scrambled eggs."

Nathan followed them into the kitchen. "Marta always makes the girls' breakfast first, but before that, she makes my coffee. Then I normally sit out on the porch drinking my coffee while the girls have their breakfast."

"Then *Dat* comes inside to have his," Grace said.

"That's right," he said smiling at Grace.

"Very well," Deborah said.

Deborah boiled the water for the coffee and then proceeded to make the girls their breakfast. The moment she put the eggs over the low heat, she took the coffee out to

Nathan. She'd given the girls the job of setting the table and hoped she could ask Nathan one of Marta's questions.

"Ah, *denke,* Deborah."

"You're welcome. I just got the girls' eggs on. It's lovely out here. It's a beautiful view."

"It is. I sit here and am grateful for what I've got and how *Gott* has blessed me. I was penniless when I was sixteen and then I worked hard to make some money and when I was a little over twenty, I lost it all and then *Gott* helped me to get what I have now. I like to sit here and appreciate Him every morning."

"That sounds like a lovely idea. And you have been blessed. You've got two amazing *dochders."*

She could tell from his face he was thinking about his late wife. Now she couldn't mention Marta. It would just be wrong.

He continued speaking when he looked out over the fields. "I'm surrounded by good people. Now I am grateful for the latest good person *Gott* has brought into my life." He looked around at her. "And that's you." He chuckled. "In case you were wondering."

"*Denke,* that's a lovely thing to say. That makes me feel good."

"I know the girls are safe with you. You've always been a sensible girl."

He looked at her with soft brown eyes and if she hadn't known any better, she would have thought he liked her. "I should see to those eggs."

"*Jah,* you should. You don't want to burn the first breakfast you cook here."

She swung around and rushed back to the kitchen and was just in time to give the eggs a good stir before they were completely cooked. The girls were already sitting at the table ready for their breakfast.

"There you are," she said as she placed a plate in front of each girl.

"*Denke,* Miss Deborah."

"Denke, Miss Deborah," the younger sister repeated.

"You're very welcome." She turned around and put strips of bacon into the pan for Nathan's breakfast.

When his breakfast was nearly cooked, he came inside and sat down at the table with the girls.

"How's the food?" he asked them.

"Really good," Emma said.

"Miss Deborah is a good cooker," Grace said.

Nathan chuckled. "You mean a good cook."

"Yeah, a good cook."

Deborah placed Nathan's breakfast in front of him.

"Denke, Deborah."

When he'd nearly finished the food, he sent the girls upstairs to finish getting ready while Deborah cleared the dishes from the table. All she felt comfortable doing on Marta's behalf was asking maybe one small question a day, otherwise it would sound like she was interrogating the poor man.

"How is the food?"

"Wunderbaar."

"Is there anything in particular you'd like me to do today?"

"Nothing that I can think of. Just general things. Do you know my *bruder* very well?"

"About the same as I know you."

"Now that you're here, I've got a funny feeling that he might come here again today since he knows that you'll be here every day."

"Maybe. He has offered to drive the girls to and from school every day. Did he mention that to you?"

"Nee, but I wouldn't count on that. He might do it once or twice and then lose interest. It's not my place to say this, but I will anyway. I wouldn't consider him a stable member of the community because he's only just come back from *rumspringa.* Who knows if he'll leave again? I wouldn't like you to become too attached to him."

CHAPTER 11

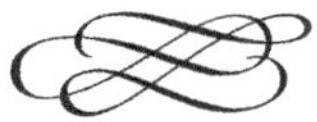

From his words, Deborah assumed that he thought she liked Adam. "I understand what you're saying. And there's no danger of that."

Nathan gave an embarrassed chuckle. "I shouldn't have said anything. None of my business, really."

"He seems pretty keen to stay on in the community and he's looking for a job."

"I hope he finds one soon."

That meant he hadn't given Adam a job.

Nathan continued, "He'll sort himself out

eventually, I'm sure, but until then it might not be a good idea to become entangled."

"I have no intention of being entangled with him or anybody else." She continued clearing dishes, hoping she didn't sound too curt and abrupt. "If he comes here, shall I tell him to leave? What would you have me do?"

"Do what you think is right at the time."

"Okay. I will. Do you mind if I ask you a personal question?"

"I don't know. I'll tell you when I hear it." He stared at her and leaned back slightly in this chair.

"Is Marta just working for you, or are the two of you engaged to marry?"

He sighed. "That is … that's a very complicated matter. I've been put in a very difficult position there. What do you do when you keep telling someone something and they just won't listen?" He covered his ears with his hands. "It's like this."

"I would tell them again and again until they understood. And I wouldn't stop telling them. Especially if it's something that's for their own good."

His gaze fell to the table and he slowly nodded as he exhaled deeply. "You're right. I'll have to make it clearer in some way." The girls came back into the kitchen ready for school just when their conversation had come to an end. "I had better get to work or I'll be late."

The two girls rushed to their father and hugged him.

Deborah had the answer for Marta; he was no longer interested in marrying her. That's why he hadn't set a date. From what he said, he'd tried to tell her and she hadn't heard the words.

She couldn't hurt Marta by telling her what he'd said, and neither could she tell Elizabeth. It was best for Marta to hear it from Nathan. Also, Marta had to know deep down in her heart the truth of the matter. If Nathan had really been in love with her, he would've set a date for the wedding and they would've been married long ago.

A little later when she was making herself cup of hot chocolate to have while she took a rest, she was sure she'd heard a buggy. She looked out the window and saw Adam coming toward the house. Just like he said he would, Adam arrived to drive the girls to school.

She was secretly pleased for the company and put the hot water back on to boil before she made her way to open the front door.

Adam grinned from ear-to-ear as he jumped down from the buggy and looked up at the front door to see her standing there. "I came to check on the new nanny."

"I'm fine."

"How about a cup of *kaffe* since I saved you a long walk when I take the girls this morning?"

"Come in. I've just put the hot water on to boil."

While Adam settled himself in the

kitchen, Deborah busied herself getting the coffee ready.

"What do you know about Marta?" he asked out of the blue.

She glanced around, wondering what he knew of the Marta/Nathan situation. "I know she's gone to look after her sick *grossmammi.*"

"That's the story I heard as well."

She placed the coffee in front of him. "I don't know where her *grossmammi* lives."

"Only about a two-hour bus ride away, so it's not far. I've got a friend who lives close by and I was thinking of going there to visit and then I found out Marta's gone there."

"That is a coincidence."

"Yeah," he said before he sipped his coffee. "This is *wunderbaar* coffee again."

"*Denke*. And you're still looking for a job here, or where your friend lives?"

"I'm looking for one wherever I can get one, but in a small town I might have a better chance of finding one."

"Do you think so? I would've thought the opposite would be true."

"We'll see, I suppose."

"Who's your friend?" she asked him.

"My friend?"

"You said you had a friend in the same town as Marta's *grossmammi."*

"Oh, that friend."

"Is that right, or do you just want to visit Marta?"

He chuckled. "Guilty."

Disappointment flooded through Deborah. Adam had been talking to her only so he could get information about Marta. Nathan had lost interest in Marta and it was odd to find out that his brother was interested in her. "Are you in love with Marta too?"

He shook his head. "Of course not."

His words weren't convincing.

"I just want to make sure she's okay. I didn't know she wouldn't be here and I haven't seen her for a long time. She's nearly part of the family, she's been with my *bruder* so long."

"*Jah,* it's been quite a while. How long has it been?"

"A little over two years."

"That is a long time. It's a wonder she's waited that long."

He stared at her. His eyes were brown like Nathan's but Nathan's were darker. "Wouldn't you wait for the man you love?"

"He'd want to have a good reason for not setting a date for the wedding, that's all I'm saying."

He chuckled. "My *bruder* often only thinks of himself."

"Well, he has got the girls he has to consider too, I suppose."

"And don't you think those girls need a *mudder?*"

"*Jah,* of course I do. Every girl needs one, and every boy too."

"Exactly. Marta's the best person for him. He can't even see it."

"I'm sure they'll work it out."

He shook his head. "How long's it been now?"

"I see what you mean."

He chuckled. When she saw how concerned he was for Marta and his nieces she was glad he didn't have a crush on Marta. He only wanted Marta and Nathan to marry.

"I take it that your *bruder* didn't offer you a job?"

"Nee, he doesn't have a job available. At least, that's what he said. We haven't gotten along for quite some time now, since way before I left on my *rumspringa."*

"Why's that?"

"He thinks I'm lazy. I admit I used to be, but I'm not now. At least, I wouldn't be if I could find someone who'd give me a job. I've got an interview this afternoon."

"Where?"

"At the fruit markets. It doesn't sound very exciting. It's not ideally what I want to do, but it's a start."

"That's right. Everybody's got to start somewhere."

"Has Nathan said anything to you about Marta?"

"Only things relating to the children, the *haus* and my job."

"I guess he wouldn't discuss anything with you."

"Do you think he has some deep dark reason why they haven't married yet?"

"Possibly. I was expecting so. I was certain they would've gotten hitched before now."

"Do you think it has anything to do with Sally?"

"Most likely. He might not want to marry again, but if that's so, he must tell Marta that he's changed his mind."

Deborah nodded, keeping to herself that he'd indicated this morning that he'd told Marta and she wouldn't listen. Now she knew Marta wasn't the only one concerned about the lengthy engagement.

"You agree then?" he asked.

"I guess I do, but it's none of my business. I don't know Marta very well, and Nathan is a grown man and can do what he wishes. And he wouldn't be happy if he knew we were discussing him and Marta."

"I've got no doubt you're right about that. Marta's a good friend of Elizabeth's, isn't she?"

"Jah, Elizabeth got married six months after Marta got engaged."

"And I've heard Elizabeth is expecting."

Deborah nodded.

"Can't you see how hard it is for Marta?" he asked.

"I would not like to be in her position."

"What are we gonna do about it?" he asked.

She pulled a face. "We?"

"You and me. We've gotta do something."

Deborah shook her head. "Keep me out of it." She drank the last mouthful of her hot chocolate, then stood and rinsed her cup out in the sink. "Stay here as long as you like, but I have cleaning to do. I'm not getting paid to sit down and talk to you."

He chuckled.

She hoped she hadn't come across as rude. She still hadn't learned how to be subtle. The only thing she knew to do was speak her mind and say things in a straightforward manner.

"How's that bike of yours doing?"

"You heard about the bike?"

He nodded.

"It's still not fixed. Elizabeth drove me here this morning."

"I'll fetch the girls from school this afternoon."

"That would be good, *denke.* Would you be finished with your job interview by then?"

He looked at the clock on the wall. "I'm due there in half an hour. It shouldn't take that long. I'm heading there right after I take the girls to school."

"*Denke*. I'd love it if you could do that. It

would save me so much time and I'd be able to get more done around the place."

"The fried chicken you cooked last night was amazing. Everyone loved it."

"*Denke,* I'm glad you liked it."

"I did." He passed his coffee cup to her and then he got up from the table. "If you and I could work together to bring Nathan and Marta to marry, that would be a good thing."

"It's best we let them sort it out for themselves. I don't see there's anything that we can do."

"You can find out what's standing in Nathan's way of happiness."

She gulped. "I could try, if you think it's best."

"Good. Just be subtle. Ask some questions, maybe ask questions about Sally."

"Oh, I wouldn't like to do that."

"I'm sure he'd like to talk about her."

Deborah wasn't so sure about that. She could only imagine the pain of losing one's marriage partner. Particularly when Nathan was left alone to raise their two daughters. Surely he'd think about his late wife every time he looked at Grace and Emma.

"I'll see you after school time."

She remembered Nathan's words about his brother being unreliable. "You'll be there, won't you? I wouldn't like them to get out of school and have to wait to be picked up."

"To put your mind at ease, I'll collect you and take you with me. We'll go to get them together, just like yesterday."

"Okay, *denke.*" She called the girls down from their room and then she walked them to the door. "Oh, don't collect them tomorrow, Adam. On Fridays Nathan does it."

He gave her a wave.

As she watched the buggy leave, she wondered whether Marta was in love with the wrong brother. He seemed to care an awful lot about her, perhaps even more so than Nathan did, Deborah thought. Or did he just like her as a friend?

The whole thing started to intrigue Deborah and she made up her mind to find out all she could from Elizabeth as soon as possible.

Deborah grabbed the broom and started sweeping the porch. While she did that, she mentally swept away all her disappointment that she was a plain woman. She wondered what it would be like to have the attention of men. It had felt good the day before when she thought Adam was interested in her, before she knew he was only trying to find out all he could about Marta.

CHAPTER 12

Deborah remembered that Friday was shopping day. The plan was that after she and Nathan took the girls to school, they would go on their way to Nathan's work. From there she'd leave him and continue to the food markets to do the weekly shopping. In the afternoon, she would pick the girls up from school and then head back to his store to collect him.

The girls were pleased to have their father drive them, and he walked with them into the school room while Deborah waited in the buggy.

When he got back, he took up the reins and pulled the buggy out onto the road. “I was quite surprised when Marta said you had accepted this job.”

“Why’s that?”

“I always thought you or Elizabeth would’ve followed in your mother’s footsteps.”

“I thought about it for a while and I went with her as a birth-helper a couple of times. It’s just not for me.”

He chuckled. "I guess it’s either the kind of thing you like, or you don’t.”

“Exactly. I was looking for a job when Elizabeth told me that Marta had to go away. I didn’t even think about looking after children as a job possibility.”

“You should. You’re very *gut* at it. The girls really like you.”

Deborah gave a little giggle. “I like them too. I suppose it helps because they know me so well from when they were younger, back when I looked after the younger children at the meetings."

"You've got your list?"

"I do."

"We generally have an easier meal on Friday nights."

Deborah nodded. That sounded good to her. "Like what?"

"Pizzas."

"Okay. It's fun making pizzas."

"Marta used to buy them already made, but if you like making them you can do that."

"I'll see what they've got at the markets."

He nodded.

HOURS LATER, when Deborah was putting the last of her shopping into the buggy, she jumped when someone tapped her shoulder. She swung around to see Maggie Miller.

"That's a lot of food for a single girl, or are you shopping for your *familye?"*

"I told you the other day I'm looking after Nathan's girls while Marta is away."

"That's right, you did tell me that. She's looking after someone you said?"

It seemed that Maggie didn't believe her.

"Marta is looking after an ill relation."

"If you're talking about her *grossmammi,* I happen to know Vonda very well and I know she's not sick at all. What I've heard is that her *granddochder's* there, very upset about something. I hope it doesn't have anything to do with you."

"Me?"

"Jah."

"Nee, not at all. You've got it all wrong. Marta was the one who asked me if I could fill in for her while she was looking after her *grossmammi."* The woman stared at her blankly. "You can ask Elizabeth if you don't believe me."

"Maybe I'll do just that."

The woman was sticking her nose into things unnecessarily and all Deborah wanted to do was ask her what business it was of hers, but that would've been rude. And that probably wouldn't have mattered because the woman was being rude to her.

Deborah took a step closer to Maggie Miller. "Maybe Vonda is fine, but I'm told that's why Marta is there and that is what I will believe until I'm told otherwise—by Marta herself. I also should point out that Nathan believes Vonda is sick and I'm sure Marta wouldn't want him to doubt her word."

She hoped the woman got her point.

Slowly, Maggie nodded. "So, you're helping Marta?"

"That's right. I have no idea what I'm helping her do, but she asked me, through Elizabeth, to help her out by looking after Emma and Grace while she's gone, so that's what I'm doing."

The woman slowly smiled. "Let me know if you need help with anything."

"I will. *Denke*."

Deborah hid her annoyance as best she could and finished loading the shopping into the back of the buggy. The woman stayed put watching her. When Deborah was finished, she turned around and said goodbye. The woman gave a weak smile and left.

As Deborah got into the buggy and took hold of the reins, she wondered why Maggie Miller was protective of Marta. Maybe she was just very fond of her, like everyone else seemed to be. What would it be like to be so popular? Deborah jiggled the reins and clicked the horse forward.

CHAPTER 13

Marta

It was just getting dark on Saturday evening when there was a knock on her grandmother's door. Marta had been lying on the couch covered in a blanket. It was too late for her grandmother to have visitors. She quickly sat and folded up the blanket, hoping it was Nathan. When she heard a male voice talking to her grandmother, happiness flooded through her and she sprang to her feet. The deep voice sounded very much like Nathan's voice. As she got close to the door, she realized it wasn't Nathan at all. It was his brother, Adam. Her grandmother had just asked him in and he stepped through the door closer to Marta.

"Adam, what are you doing here?"

"I'll be in the kitchen," her grandmother said as she made herself scarce.

"I've come to check on you, to make sure you're okay."

"I'm fine."

"Your *grossmammi* is the one who looks fine to me."

"Come and sit with me." She pushed the front door closed and they both made their way to the living room. When she sat down, he sat on the couch next to her. She moved herself away from him a little in case her grandmother would think that she was sitting too close to him. "You shouldn't have come all this way."

"It's not that far. I had to see you. I've

been waiting a good several months to see you. You should know by now he has no intention of marrying you, but I will."

She shook her head. "We've talked about this before."

"*Jah,* we talked about it two years ago, and now everything's different."

She looked away from him. She knew she was the reason he had left the community, because he couldn't stand to see her with his brother. It was a difficult choice to make between the two of them, the hardest she'd ever have to make. With Nathan, she had stability and a ready-made family, and someone needed to look after the girls. Adam, on the other hand, didn't show the same stability and didn't know what he wanted out of life. "I made a commitment to your *bruder.*"

"I think the time has expired on your commitment to him. How long is he going to wait for the actual marriage?"

"I don't know," she said in a small voice. At this point, she figured the best solution was total honesty. "I want a large family and you don't even have a job to support yourself."

"*Bopplis* don’t come all at once. They come one by one. We’ll adjust to that and so will my income. Anyway, a lot of people have a lot of *kinner* and barely any money."

"I want to enjoy my *kinner.* I don't want to worry about money and never be able to enjoy them or anything else. That's how I was raised. It was like living with a black cloud hanging over us all of the time. My *mudder* had to scrimp and save to get by. She was so busy earning a little money by cooking and sewing for other families that she barely had time to talk to us. We had to raise ourselves."

He shook his head. "I'm sorry, Marta. I didn't know that.”

“It was like that until I was thirteen and my father got a better job. Then we were a lot better off, but I'll never forget the struggle as they tried to feed all of us. I can't, and I won't go through that again."

"Trust me, I'll be able to provide for you, me and all of our *kinner*—however many *Gott* blesses us with."

She looked into his pleading eyes and wanted to believe him. He'd been her first choice but at the time she'd thought Nathan the better choice. Then her mind leaned toward Nathan, and her heart followed. The best provider and the most favorable man to be her husband was Nathan, so she'd thought. It made sense because he'd already proven he was a wonderful father and a good provider. "You don't even have a job now, do you?"

"I'm waiting to hear about a job."

She shook her head. "Waiting to hear about one won't pay the bills."

"I'll come back to you when I have a job."

"It won't do any good because I made a commitment to Nathan."

"You keep saying that, Marta, but he

hasn't fulfilled his commitment to you." He reached out and grabbed her hand and at that moment, she desperately wanted to be held in his arms.

A long time ago, she'd had to steel her heart against him to give herself the best chance in life. Now that same sense of self-preservation returned and she pulled her hand away. "Stop it, Adam."

"I can't! When will you realize you've made a commitment to the wrong *bruder?* He's not for you."

"I don't think there are any wrong choices in life. There are simply different paths to walk along. I chose to go along the path toward Nathan and not you. Why can't you just accept that?"

"'Why?' You ask me why?"

She nodded.

"Because I'm in love with you, Marta. You're the first thing on my mind every morning, and as I close my eyes at night your face is right there. I've never been able to get you out of my head and believe me, I've tried. We'd be so good together. We'd be a great team."

"I don't want to be a team. I want someone to look after me and I've chosen Nathan as that person."

He bounded to his feet. "I'm sorry for wasting your time."

She stood as well. "Where are you staying?"

"I'm staying with a friend. I'll head back tomorrow." He started walking to the door and she followed close behind. She reached out for the doorknob trying to get there before he did. As she touched it, his warm hand covered hers. She looked up into his eyes and the two of them shared a moment as though frozen in time. She could no longer bear the weight of keeping up those tall fences that surrounded her heart. He lowered his head and whispered in her ear. "I love you, Marta, with everything that is within me."

Many emotions swirled in her body. Love—Nathan had never said he'd loved her. Tingles ran through her as his soft warm breath tickled her cheek. With the edge of his finger he tilted her chin back. Their eyes locked and again she was frozen to the spot. Adam's gaze traveled from her eyes to her lips, and he lowered his lips against hers. Her heart pounded with anticipation as she savored the softness and gentleness of his kiss.

Good sense finally prevailed and she pulled herself away and stepped back. *"Nee!"*

He put his hands down by his side and when she looked back into his eyes she could see how deeply hurt he was.

"Goodbye, Marta." His voice was a soft whisper barely heard. He pulled the door open and walked away.

She opened the door wider, staring after him. Now she knew what it was like to be truly loved. How was it she had feelings for Adam and for Nathan too? Was it possible to love two men?

With the tips of her fingers. she touched the exact place he'd kissed her. Had she chosen the wrong brother two years ago? If she'd chosen Adam, she could've been married with one or two *kinner* by now. She closed the door.

CHAPTER 14

Deborah

It was Saturday before Deborah could talk to Elizabeth again. She borrowed the family buggy and paid her sister a visit.

Peter was already at work and Deborah knocked on the front door. "Hello!"

"Come in," Elizabeth called out from inside the house.

Deborah pushed the door open and saw Elizabeth sitting on the couch, sewing.

“Close the door and come sit with me.” As soon as Deborah sat down, Elizabeth asked, "Did you ask Nathan the questions?”

“I asked a question or two and didn’t really find anything out.”

Elizabeth leaned forward. “Didn’t really?”

Elizabeth was no fool. She was very hard to put one over on. Deborah didn’t want to betray Nathan by telling Elizabeth that he’d more or less said he’d tried to speak to Marta about things but she wouldn’t listen. Her plan today was getting information from Elizabeth. “I’m here because I want to know what’s really going on. Adam’s back from *rumspringa.* I don’t know if you know that.”

“I’ve heard he was back.”

“He seems very concerned for Marta’s welfare, and I was wondering if there was more going on between them than just a friendship.” When Elizabeth stopped sewing and looked at her blankly, Deborah said, "I need to know the whole truth if you want me to help Marta.”

Elizabeth sighed. "Okay, I'll tell you everything but you must keep it all to yourself. Agreed?"

"Agreed."

Elizabeth began her story and Deborah had her eyes glued onto her. "Going back around two and a half years ago, Adam and Marta had dated a couple of times and all was going well. But then she began to fall in love with Nathan."

That's what Deborah had suspected. "That must've been disappointing for Adam. You mean, just like that, she started falling in love with Nathan?"

"It happens like that sometimes."

"Is that why the brothers don't get along?" Deborah asked.

"Don't they?"

"I sensed tension when Adam came there for dinner the other night—the first night I was there."

"I guess there could be tension between them. Adam had to watch his girlfriend fall in love with his *bruder* and had to step aside. Now two years later, Nathan still hasn't married Marta. Adam is probably wondering why he gave up on her."

"I see what you mean. *Jah,* that makes perfect sense."

Elizabeth looked back at her sewing. "So, there you have it. Now you know everything."

"Everything? You haven't told me that Marta has gone away to have a break from the situation in the hope that Nathan misses her enough to make a date for the wedding," Deborah stated. "I've had to guess that for myself."

"Jah, that's what she's done. I hope it all works out for her. She's my very best friend and she's such a nice person."

Deborah couldn't comment on that because she'd never spent much time with Marta. Marta hadn't seemed like a very friendly person to her, or perhaps that's because over the past two years she'd been stressed about her relationship with Nathan. Besides that, Marta had told Elizabeth she'd leave Deborah a list to tell her exactly how to care for Nathan's household and she hadn't done so. Was that just because Marta was so stressed, or had it been done to deliberately make Deborah look bad to Nathan?

"What do you think's going on there? Why hasn't he set a date for the wedding? Has he changed his mind?" Deborah wanted to give Elizabeth a hint and that way wasn't betraying Nathan's trust.

Elizabeth shook her head. "No one knows. That's what I was hoping you would find out."

"Me?"

"Yep."

Deborah said, "Has she ever just asked him outright? That's what I would do."

"I suggested that and she said she can't. She was the one who asked him about getting married, so she can't set a date as well. It would be like she was instigating everything and he was just going along with it."

"Jah, I can see now that she's in a very difficult position. I can't believe a beautiful woman like Marta had to propose to a man."

Elizabeth leaned back in her chair and placed her hands on her belly. "What would you do if you were in her shoes?"

"The sensible thing would be to walk away from the situation. There's a reason he hasn't set a date and he's the one who has to sort that out."

"But what if Marta doesn't want to leave him?"

"I still think she should. It's already been two whole years. What if it drags on for two more?"

"I'll tell her you said that."

Deborah stared at her sister in disbelief. *"Nee,* don't! Don't you bring me into it any more than I am already. You've made me feel like a spy and have put me in a very difficult position. Don't you say a thing!"

"I wasn't serious."

"It's not funny."

"Relax! I won't say a thing. I appreciate everything you're doing and so does Marta. If I could do anything to help her I would, but I can't in my condition." She stared at her belly.

It was a very convenient excuse. "If you weren't expecting, what would you do to help?"

"I'm not sure, but I'd do something."

"What about the bishop? Can Marta talk to the bishop about the situation?"

"That would be too embarrassing for Nathan if anything was said. It's not as though he's an eighteen-year-old, needing the bishop to sort things out in his life and give advice to him."

"Nee, but it's probably something to do with Sally. Maybe Nathan doesn't want to start over again with another woman. Or, he might feel that Sally wouldn't want another woman helping raise her *kinner."*

"Marta's helping raise his *kinner* now."

"But that's different because he's paying her." As soon as the words came out of her mouth, Deborah regretted them. That was something that Elizabeth didn't know.

"He's not paying her, though. Wait a minute, he's paying her?"

Deborah pressed her lips together.

Elizabeth sighed. "That's not what she told me. She must feel dreadful, like she's just a paid worker. She didn't even tell me that, and I'm her closest friend."

"I should've kept my mouth shut. I didn't mean to say anything."

"Well, it's a surprise. She made out like she wasn't being paid. That puts a different slant on the whole thing."

Deborah felt bad for Marta, but the situation was as she suspected. There had been some kind of a love relationship between Adam and Marta. "I should get the buggy home in case *Mamm* needs it."

"Massage my feet?"

"*Nee,* I won't."

"Go on. They're so sore from carrying all this weight."

"Mine are sore from doing a lot of walking. Just live with it. Better yet, get your husband to massage them."

Elizabeth giggled. "It was worth a try."

CHAPTER 15

For something different, Deborah decided to take one of the back roads home. It was a little longer, but it was a more pleasant drive. When she turned a corner on the quiet road, she was surprised to see police cars gathered with a group of motorbikes and one Amish buggy. She slowed her horse to a walk, wondering if an Amish person was in trouble. As she slowly traveled past the scene, she saw a young Amish man being reprimanded by a huge policeman. On looking closer, she was shocked. It was Joshua! She quickly pulled her horse to the side of the road and secured him, and then hurried back to see what was going on. Before she reached her brother, she saw Nathan Beiler striding to intercept her.

"What's going on?"

"Your *bruder's* in a lot of trouble. He and some other boys were caught racing motorbikes and the one Joshua was on had been stolen."

Deborah gasped. No one in the family had ever been in trouble with the law before. No one had done one thing wrong. Her younger brother had ruined the family's good name.

"I'll sort this out. You go home," he said.

"Nee, I must stay!" She stared at Joshua with conflicting emotions of anger and protectiveness as the police officer towered over him.

"Go home, Deborah. I've got this. I used

to get Adam out of scrapes like this all the time."

She looked around. "Where are the girls?"

"I was just coming back home from taking them to their grandmother's for the day."

Now focusing back on her brother, she asked, "What's going to happen? Has he been arrested?"

"Not yet. Go home, and I'll bring him home later."

"You'll stay with him?"

"*Jah,* I'll look after him. You can trust me! I've been through it all before."

She stood there biting her lip, not knowing what to do.

"Go home and don't mention any of this to your folks, it'll only worry them. I'll tell them everything when I bring him home." He shooed her with his hands. She glanced over at Joshua again. He looked thoroughly miserable. He didn't need his big sister right now.

"*Denke,* Nathan."

"Don't worry, everything will be all right."

She took a step backward.

"Are you going to be okay?"

She slowly nodded. "I'll do what you said."

"Good." He turned around and strode back to Joshua and the police officers.

Deborah went back to her buggy and continued her drive home, all the while worried about the outcome. What if he was arrested and put in jail? Joshua would be scared and everyone would find out. Then she hoped the police would be lenient with him due to his young age. But he did need to learn a lesson from this.

She knew when she got home she would have to act as though nothing was wrong. If she looked weird or distracted, they would know something was wrong.

After she unhitched the buggy and rubbed the horse down, she headed into the house.

It appeared that just her sister was home.

"You left early," Jenny said as she munched on an apple.

"I was visiting Elizabeth."

"Why didn't you tell me? I would've come with you."

"You were still fast asleep when I left."

"Wake me next time," Jenny said.

Deborah looked around. "I will. Where are *Mamm* and *Dat?"*

"*Mamm* is off delivering a *boppli* somewhere, and *Dat's* helping someone mend a door on his barn."

"How did *Mamm* get there?"

"Taxi."

"Now I feel dreadful for taking the buggy."

"Nee, don't worry. She had to get there quick so she'd have gone by taxi anyway."

"Oh good. How did *Dat* get to where he had to go?"

"Someone came to get him." She took another bite of her apple and then followed

Deborah up the stairs to Deborah's room. "What are we gonna do today?"

"I'm going to have a rest." Deborah sat down on her bed thinking about Joshua and hoping he'd be okay. She hadn't asked where Joshua was and Jenny hadn't noticed that. Joshua was mostly off with his friends anyway, something that would probably change now with him being in trouble with the police.

Jenny sat down on the bed next to her. "I was hoping you could drive me into town or something. Something exciting. I'm tired of staying home all the time. Maybe I should get a job."

"You're a little young."

"I'll soon be old enough to get a job."

"That's true. What would you do?"

"I'm not sure. I've been thinking about it, and I haven't come up with anything yet. The only thing I can think of is doing what *Mamm* does. Elizabeth said I can go to her birth to see what it's like. The only thing is it's a big responsibility. It's not something where you can make a mistake."

"I suppose you could just assist *Mamm* for a few years and then you'd be confident. Then you'd obviously need some other kind of medical training, but *Mamm* would know all that."

"Why didn't you want to do that?"

"I don't know. Just because I'm not interested in something doesn't mean that you can't do it. It just wasn't for me."

"I'll start with Elizabeth's birth first."

"Good idea."

"What's it like working for Nathan Beiler?"

"It's good. The girls are lovely and so cute."

"It would be good fun to play with them."

"I don't get a lot of time to play with them. As soon as I get there I start work."

"It wouldn't be too hard."

"It's the work of a *mudder.*"

"Exactly, and they don't have one of those. When do you get paid?"

"I was paid yesterday."

Jenny's face beamed. "How much?"

"None of your business."

"What will you do with all the money?"

"I'm saving it."

"I think you should buy me something."

Deborah giggled. "And exactly what would I buy?"

"Material for a new dress."

"You've got plenty of dresses."

"I can always do with a new one."

"That's what your parents are for."

Jenny sighed. "Unfair. We've got the buggy all to ourselves for the first time in ages, so why can't we go out somewhere?"

She couldn't tell her sister that they couldn't go out anywhere because Nathan might be bringing Joshua home at any time. She only hoped that her parents were both there when that happened. Otherwise, she wouldn't know what to say to Joshua. "I just want to relax today if that's okay with you."

"Boring! You should've told me you were going to Elizabeth's. Why can't you take me back there now?"

"I'm fairly certain she was going out somewhere."

Jenny sighed again. "I'm going to my room to write some letters."

CHAPTER 16

Marta

Marta opened her eyes and was glad that Saturday morning had finally come. She had barely gotten any sleep thinking about Adam's kiss. Nathan had never kissed her, never tried to kiss her. When she heard noises in the kitchen, she changed out of her nightdress and went to join her grandmother for breakfast. Her grandmother had the habit of eating breakfast at first light.

When she walked in to see her grandmother fully dressed and looking bright, she felt bad about telling people her grandmother was ill. It had been a quick lie, but a dreadful one and she regretted it.

" *Guder mariye."* Her grandmother looked up to see her staggering into the kitchen.

Marta stifled a yawn and slumped into a chair. *"Guder mariye, Mammi."*

"You look like you didn't get much sleep."

"I didn't get any. Well, not much."

"Does that have anything to do with your visitor last night?"

She looked at her grandmother. "It has everything to do with him."

"You'll have to tell me over a cup of hot tea."

"You sit. I'll make it."

"I'll do it. I had some sleep."

"Denke. I don't know what to do, *Mammi.* Adam said he wants to marry me."

She swung her head around. "Adam?"

"Jah, Adam."

"That's a change. What would his *bruder* have to say about that?"

"He probably wouldn't even care. I've been here for days and he hasn't even called."

Her grandmother put the teakettle on the stove and turned on the gas. "Does he have the number?"

"Jah, I made sure he had it."

When she sat back down, she said, "He probably doesn't want to disturb you."

Marta shrugged. "Or it could be that he's pleased to have a break from me."

"It wouldn't be that."

"I'm not so sure. Adam said he wants to marry me and as soon as I agree he said we'll get married right away."

Her grandmother shifted uncomfortably in her chair.

"So, what do you think, *Mammi?* I know you have an opinion about everything."

"It's your choice to make. "

"I know that, but I value your opinion."

She looked down at the table for a long

time before she spoke. "You can't tell me that you love both brothers the same. Maybe you were once fond of them equally, but no one can truly love two men the same. You need to make the choice before anyone gets hurt."

She wondered if that's what was happening—she loved the two men equally, but for different reasons. "What if I do love them both the same?"

"Nonsense. I've never heard of such a thing."

"I chose Nathan because he has his own business and is stable, and Adam doesn't even have a job. And he left the community." She knew she wasn't being fair to Adam, because she knew he left the community due to being upset over her. If she had chosen him, he would've stayed.

"Has Adam been baptized now?"

"I'm sure he'll do that soon. He said he's back to stay. He's had his *rumspringa*."

"That's a start."

"So, what do you think?"

"You have to follow your heart. I can't tell you what to do."

"It's not as easy as that. I don't want to be poor like we were when I was growing up. I saw how *Mamm* and *Dat* worried that they wouldn't have enough food for us."

"There were a lot of families like that back then. It wasn't unusual. Times are different now. The whole community where you live is more prosperous. If one family falls, the other families help with food and everything."

"I don't want to be helped."

"You'd rather be one of those families who helps others rather than be helped?"

"That's right, that's it exactly."

Her grandmother pulled a face. "Marta, that's just foolish pride!"

"I don't know if looking after yourself and your family properly is called pride."

"It depends on how far you take it. Sometimes *Gott* wants us to let others help us for a time, to teach others to be generous and us to be humble."

When the kettle whistled, Marta stood to make the tea. "I suppose we could go back and forth arguing about this for a long time."

"We're not arguing we're simply having a discussion."

Marta poured the hot water into the teapot. "I'm so confused."

"Why are you hanging onto Nathan when he hasn't even set a date for the wedding? If you want my honest opinion, he's not taking your needs or wants into consideration. And, as you said, he hasn't made the effort to call you while you've been here. Isn't that telling you something?"

"I guess it is." She placed a teacup and saucer in front of her grandmother and got a set out for herself. Then she sat down.

"Denke, Marta." She picked up the cup of hot tea and took a sip.

"What you say is true, and that's what I've

been scared of, but now I have to accept that Nathan doesn't want me."

"Don't feel bad. You'll find someone who wants to marry you."

She frowned at *Mammi.* "I already have, and I've been pushing him out of my heart for too long."

"Why don't we go out somewhere for lunch today?"

"Really?"

"Why not?"

"I'd love that."

"We'll go down by the riverside. There's a nice eating place where we can sit and watch the water."

"I'd like that." Marta felt that something had shifted; she now felt as though she could go out in public. She'd been wise to come to *Mammi's.*

CHAPTER 17

Deborah

Deborah had tried to keep herself busy as best she could by sewing her sampler. She hadn't touched that sampler in six months and had lost interest in it. Now she was too nervous to do anything else. She couldn't just sit there and do nothing and she was overwhelmed with the burden of hoping she'd done the right thing in leaving Joshua in Nathan's hands.

Nathan had said he'd gotten Adam out of

trouble in his youth. What kind of trouble, Deborah wondered.

Perhaps she should've found her father and told him what had happened and let him go to the police station to sort it all out. But could stealing a motorbike be sorted out? Surely Joshua would be charged, and he might even go to jail or some youth facility.

Three hours after Deborah had arrived home, she heard a clunking wagon. She flung the door open to see her father being brought to the house in a friend's wagon. Now he'd ask where Joshua was and she couldn't say she didn't know because she did. To her relief, she noticed Nathan's buggy coming up fast behind the slow wagon. Squinting, she saw Joshua in the seat next to him. Finally she could relax.

She stepped back inside the house and watched from the living room window as the scene unfolded. Nathan got out of his buggy and headed over to talk to her father while Joshua got out of Nathan's buggy but stayed close by it. Deborah could only imagine how fearful Joshua would be about their father finding out about the stolen motorbike.

She saw the look on her father's face at the point where Nathan would've been explaining what had happened. When he looked over at his son, Joshua looked down at the ground. Nathan continued talking and soon she saw her father nod, and Nathan called Joshua over.

Her father said a few words to Joshua, and then Joshua said a few words and their father pointed to the house. Joshua turned and walked to the house. Her brother opened the door, stepped inside, closed it, and then ran upstairs without even looking at Deborah. He probably hadn't noticed her there. She wondered if she should go out and thank Nathan, but she didn't know what mood her father would be in. She saw him thank Nathan. The two men shook hands and Nathan returned to his buggy. She stepped away from the window in case Nathan glanced back at the house.

Once she heard Nathan's buggy leave, she walked out to her father. "What's going on?"

He shook his head. "Your *bruder* decided to steal a motorbike. It was a good thing Nathan came on the scene when the police had caught up with him. Nathan was able to talk to the owner of the bike, and he didn't press charges."

"So, Joshua's not going to get into trouble?"

"Not from the police. Where's your *mudder?"*

"She's been called out."

He grunted. "Have you started dinner?"

Dinner? She'd forgotten all about dinner. "Jenny and I will put it on now."

"Good. You do that while I have a few words with Joshua."

CHAPTER 18

Marta

When Marta arrived at the Sunday church meeting with her grandmother, she looked around in surprise at how much the church had grown in numbers. It had doubled in size since she'd been there a few years ago. Someone there would say something and it would be almost certain that word would get back to Nathan that there was nothing wrong with her grandmother.

As soon as they were seated in the home where the meeting was being held, she was surprised to see Adam walk into the house. He gave her grandmother a quick nod, and another to her, and then sat on the other side of the room with the men.

She was positive from the way their conversation had ended that he would've left her alone, but he was still here.

When the meeting was over, Marta was outside the house talking to some of *Mammi's* friends. She knew that Adam was lurking behind her waiting to speak with her. She excused herself from the ladies and turned around to face him. He smiled at her and together they walked a few steps away so no one could hear them.

"What are you still doing here?" she hissed.

"I told you I'm visiting a friend."

She looked around. "Who's your friend?"

"All right, I'm staying at a nearby bed and

breakfast. I just had to see you one more time."

His words pleased her, she realized.

"I'm leaving tomorrow morning, and I'll go back home. And I'll wait for you there."

"I don't want you to wait for me. We've talked about it so many times. I'm done talking about things."

"Exactly what do you want, Marta?"

"I just want to be happy, that's all."

"We'll be happy together. I'll make sure of it."

She glanced around making sure no one could hear them. "You don't even have a job."

"I'll get one."

"And then what will we do, live with your *mudder?*"

"If you agree to marry me maybe we'll have to live with her for a few months. We'll be together; isn't that all that matters?"

She sighed. "I told you, I'm fearful of putting children through what I went through, and that won't change."

"Trust in *Gott* and trust in me. I've now been baptized, and I'm reliable. You won't have to ever be in that situation again."

She didn't trust him, but she wanted to. Her gaze fell to the ground.

He whispered, "Look at me, Marta."

She stared into his eyes.

"I will provide for us. I will get a job tomorrow, as soon as I can, and then I'll get us a *haus.* I will prove myself to you. Don't marry anyone but me."

"You don't have to prove yourself to me."

"From everything you're saying, it seems I do. Now I know that's why you chose Nathan over me. You're in love with me, but you want the money and security he can give you."

She looked down at the ground again, ashamed of herself. What he said was the truth, but saying it so succinctly made her feel like she was too focused on money and material possessions. It wasn't like that. She could live without the best of everything, what she wanted—no, what she needed—was to have the basic needs met.

Marta put a hand over her stomach. "I'm not feeling the best." All she wanted to do was run away from him, and run away from everyone, and hide under a blanket in her grandmother's living room. "Excuse me, Adam." She walked away from him and rejoined her grandmother's friends in their conversation about quilting.

CHAPTER 19

Deborah

When the Sunday meeting was over and everyone was eating the meal that followed, she waited until Nathan was alone and then approached him. "What happened at the police station yesterday?"

"Everything was settled, there's no need to worry."

"*Denke* for everything you've done. I was so worried. Exactly what did you do?"

"I talked with the owner of the motorbike, and he agreed not to press charges. He said he'd been silly in his younger years as well and had done a similar thing. He wasn't too annoyed, and there were just a few scratches on the bike which Joshua has agreed to pay for."

"How will he do that? I doubt *Dat* will give him the money."

"I already paid the man what he guessed it would take to fix it. It wasn't a large amount, and Joshua will come to my place to do jobs until that is paid off. I've already arranged it with your *vadder.*"

Deborah giggled. "And Joshua agreed to it?"

Nathan smiled. "He didn't have much choice."

"It was nice of you to do that for him."

"As I said, I'm used to it because of my Adam."

"It sounds like Adam was a bit of a handful when he was Joshua's age."

"You don't know the half of it. He was always getting out of one situation and into another."

"He turned out okay," Deborah said.

"I guess he did."

Now that she had the opportunity, it was her turn to help someone. "Have you spoken to Marta since she's been away?"

"I haven't. I've been meaning to call. Maybe I'll do that this afternoon."

"I think she'd like that. Are you pleased with the job I'm doing? Please tell me if you want me to do things differently. I'm doing my best, but it's hard because I'm not sure if you … If I'm doing everything you want me to do."

"You're doing fine. The girls are happy and well looked after, and I come home to a lovely meal, and the place is clean and tidy. What more could I ask?"

His words pleased Deborah. "I'm so relieved."

"I'm surprised the girls have taken to you so well."

"They're such good girls. They're so easy to look after, and they play so well together."

"It helps that they're only two years apart."

"I guess so."

They were interrupted when Jenny tugged on her arm. "*Mamm* said you have to come and help in the kitchen."

What rotten timing. She just wanted to stay there talking with Nathan. She still liked him as she'd done as a young girl, and now that she was grown up, a small part of her wanted to imagine that he didn't want to marry Marta and he'd fallen in love with her.

She looked back at Nathan. "Excuse me; I guess I'll have to go and help."

"I'll see you tomorrow morning, Deborah."

"Come on, Deborah, *Mamm's* waiting."

"Bye, Nathan." She turned around and walked to the house with her sister. "I was talking. That was rude of you to interrupt me."

"What could you possibly have to talk about? You see him every day."

"For your information, we were talking about Joshua. I was thanking him for helping out."

"Why would you thank him? *Mamm* and *Dat* already thanked him."

"It doesn't hurt to be polite. Something you could take a lesson or two on."

"You've been really bossy ever since you got that job." Her sister flounced into the house before her.

She turned around to have another look at Nathan, he was as handsome as ever. Then she looked down at herself and visualized how she would look to Nathan after him being used to seeing the slim and beautiful Marta. There was no comparison. Even if she lost all the extra weight, she'd never be as beautiful.

Then a thought occurred to her. Where

was Adam? She couldn't remember him being seated during the meeting. She looked around the yard for Adam, but he was nowhere to be seen. Had he left the community again, so soon after coming back?

On Monday morning, Joshua joined her on her journey to Nathan's house. Today was his first day of doing jobs for Nathan to pay him back for the damage on the motorcycle. Joshua was on foot while Deborah rode her bike alongside him.

"Can't I ride the bike?"

"There's no way. Besides, you're used to walking everywhere."

"I only walk when I have to."

"Well, you have to now."

"Go a little slower, I can't keep up."

"Run a little."

"You're enjoying seeing me suffer, aren't you?"

"*Jah*, I am." Deborah laughed. "Why did

you do something silly like stealing that motorbike?"

"I just wanted bit of excitement, that's all."

"Who were the kids you were racing?"

"Just people you don't know."

"Were they from the community?"

"I can't say. My lips are sealed."

"What do you feel about that excitement now—the excitement that nearly landed you in jail?"

"I didn't think that far ahead."

"Thinking ahead is part of being an adult."

"Yeah well, I'm just a kid."

"Yeah, a kid who was nearly sent to a correctional facility. How much excitement do you think that would've been?"

"Yeah, I know. I've heard it all before from M and D."

"M and D?"

"Mamm and *Dat."*

"Oh. I should've been able to figure that one out."

"Do you know what Nathan is going to have me do?"

"Nee." When the house came into view, Deborah pedalled harder, leaving Joshua panting behind her.

"Wait up!"

"Run faster," she called over her shoulder. She was enjoying the payback for him twisting her wheel.

When she stopped her bike, the girls were waiting for her at the window. When she opened the front door, they ran to hug her like they normally did.

"Good morning, where's your *vadder?"*

Emma said, "He's in the *haus* somewhere."

When she looked back at Joshua, she felt a little bad when she saw him puffing with bright red cheeks. She could have shared her bike with him.

At that moment, Nathan walked down the stairs. He greeted Deborah and she told him Joshua was outside waiting for instructions from him.

She left Nathan to talk to Joshua and she went into the kitchen with the girls to cook their breakfast.

"What's your *bruder* doing here, Miss Deborah?"

"He's helping your *vadder* by doing some jobs."

"What kind of jobs?" Grace asked.

Before she could answer the question, Emma asked, "Why is he doing jobs for *Dat?"*

"To answer both of you, I don't know what kind of jobs he's doing and Joshua likes helping people."

She put the hot water on for Nathan's coffee and then cracked eggs into a bowl. "Are you both ready for school?"

Grace looked down at her feet. "I just have to put my shoes on."

"She can't find them," Emma said.

"Well, you both better go looking and find them now. Hurry before I have breakfast on the table."

"It's no use, we've already looked," Emma said, puffing out her chubby cheeks.

"Look under your beds. They have to be somewhere."

The two girls hurried out of the room. Once she had the eggs on the stove, she made the coffee and took a cup out to the porch where Nathan usually drank it. He was still talking to Joshua by the barn so she left his coffee on the table beside his usual chair. "Coffee is here," she called out to Nathan and he responded by giving her a wave.

Nathan helping Joshua like he had just made Deborah like him even more.

CHAPTER 20

Marta

By Monday morning, things had become quite clear to Marta. Being with her grandmother had been nice for a few days, but now she had to go back and make some tough life decisions. If her substitute was doing fine looking after Nathan's household and being a nanny to his children, there was no reason why Deborah couldn't continue in that role. Hopefully, Deborah would be able to stay on rather than the girls having to get used to another nanny. Then it occurred to Marta that if she was no longer going to marry Nathan, the girls were no longer her concern.

Now she knew that Nathan was never going to marry her, and that fact had been brought home to her clearly by his not bothering to call her in all the time that she had been at her grandmother's. He could've at least called out of politeness to check that she'd arrived. It was hurtful that he didn't care. The last two years of her life had been a waste, caring for someone's children who would never really be hers. Even if Nathan apologized and threw himself at her feet, she wouldn't forgive those last two years spent in limbo while hoping he'd make a date for their nuptials. It was unfair of him to have put her through that. If he had no intention of marrying her, he should've told her that from the beginning.

Anger rose within her, anger that she'd been holding back for two years. She wanted to confront him and let him know exactly what she thought of him. She would spend the next day or two enjoying her grandmother's company and then she'd return home.

It was Thursday night when Marta knocked on Nathan's door. She knew she had arrived at a time the girls would be in bed. She needed to have a serious talk with him alone.

He opened the door and was surprised to see her. "Marta, you're back!"

"I am."

"How's your *grossmammi?"*

"She's fine. Can I come in?"

He stepped aside. "Of course."

She walked past him, made her way to the living room and sat down on the couch. He sat in front of her. "You didn't even call me the whole time I was away."

He raised his eyebrows. "You haven't been gone that long."

“Did you miss me?"

"Of course I missed you."

"What’s happening with us?"

"In what way?"

"Our relationship?" As soon as she asked that question she knew it was all over. She had dropped to a new low-point, having to ask that question.

He scratched his head. "I told you that the first time you mentioned marriage, that I wasn't ready."

She was taken aback. "I don't remember that."

"I told you it was too soon for me. Although I do feel some affection for you, it will take some more time before I'm ready to give myself to another woman. Do you understand that?"

He had never said that he loved her and now he only said he had some affection for her. That wasn't love. That wasn't anything like love. "So, you don't love me?"

"As I said, it will take me some time to feel that again."

And that was her answer. "I need to tell you that your *bruder* has proposed to me and I'm thinking of accepting his offer."

His eyebrows drew together. "Adam wants to marry you?"

She nodded.

"Right now, I have nothing to offer you."

"Do you think I should accept Adam's proposal?"

"If that's what you want."

“Well, what do you want?" Now that she was in his house in front of him, it was harder than she’d thought it would be to let go. He had everything that she imagined her husband would have. He was a hard-working man, kind, caring, good looking, and he was wonderful with children. But he didn't love her.

"Like I said, I can't offer you anything at this time. Maybe in a few years." He swallowed hard.

"I can see I'm wasting my time here." She bounded to her feet. "I can no longer work here for you."

"I'm sorry, but I thought you knew where things were between us." He stood.

"Do you think that Deborah will stay on?"

"I could ask her."

"Then you should do that." Without saying anything further, Marta walked out of the house, got into her buggy and drove into the night.

Tears streamed down her face as soon as she was well away from the house. Whether they were tears of relief or tears of disappointment, she didn't know. Deep down within her heart was a small sense of resolution that she finally knew they'd never marry. When she got closer to her home, she dried her tears on her sleeve. Not knowing her future with Nathan had been horrible, but at least now she knew.

CHAPTER 21

Deborah

Fridays were Deborah's favorite day. It was the day she got time to be alone with Nathan while she rode with him to work. This particular day was the last day of Joshua working off his money for the damaged bike. After Nathan and Deborah had taken the girls to school, they continued to Nathan's work. From there, Deborah would do the weekly shopping. It was also the day she got paid, which was another reason she liked Fridays.

As the buggy clip-clopped down the road, Nathan turned to her. "How would you like this job to become permanent?"

"I would love that, but won't Marta be back soon?"

"She's back already. She came to the *haus* last night and told me she no longer wants to ... She no longer wants to continue doing what she was doing."

"Oh, I'm sorry to hear that. I would love to stay on if that's all right with you."

He took his eyes off the road and smiled at her. "I'd like that very much. Your presence has brought peace to the household."

Deborah giggled. "Do you mean that?"

"*Jah,* you have a lovely soothing, calming personality, and that's an influence I would like around the girls more often."

"*Denke,* that's nice of you to say."

They traveled a little further in silence. There were one million things running around in Deborah's mind. It had to mean that the relationship between him and Marta had been called off. She'd find out soon enough from Elizabeth. Who had broken up with whom? That's what she wanted to know, merely because she was inquisitive. "Would you like anything in particular from the markets today?"

"Whatever you think we'll need."

When they arrived at his work, he got out, and she changed into the driver's seat. He handed her the wages for the week, and money for the shopping.

Some months later on a Friday night, Peter had called to tell the Fisher family that Elizabeth was in the early stages of labor. Mr. Fisher stayed home while *Mamm,* Deborah and Jenny went to assist with the birth. Deborah was there for moral support while their younger sister was also going to assess whether she wanted to entertain a career in midwifery.

ELIZABETH AND PETER'S child was born early on that Saturday morning. It was a girl and Peter wanted to name their brand new daughter after Elizabeth, but Elizabeth wasn't so keen on the idea. They ended up agreeing to name the child Elizabeth, but to call her Liz for short.

When Deborah's turn finally came to hold the baby, it was an odd feeling to hold the next generation in her arms. Tears came to her eyes, which Jenny pointed out and laughed about. *Mamm* quickly put an end to that, reminding Jenny that new babies brought out all sorts of emotions. Deborah sniffed and didn't care who saw her tears of joy. She was happy to have a niece, and happy for her older sister and Peter to have the first addition to their family.

. . .

THE NEXT DAY at the meeting, Deborah couldn't wait to tell Nathan about her baby niece. The girls, Emma and Grace, sat at the front of the house with their grandmother, while Nathan sat on the men's side of the room.

At the end of the meeting, the bishop announced to everybody that Peter and Elizabeth had a new baby girl. Now that she had no reason to talk to Nathan, Deborah was disappointed. It was then she realized that she was in trouble. She really liked Nathan, and she knew she'd have to keep that to herself and not tell anybody.

At the meal after the meeting, out in the yard, Nathan approached her.

"Congratulation on your baby niece."

"*Denke.* I was there for the birth. I was the fourth person to hold her."

"That's a wonderful feeling. I'm glad she's healthy, and everything went well."

"It did. Everything went smoothly."

"I know you spend nearly every day with us, but the girls and I were wondering if you might come on a picnic with us when the meeting is finished? That is, if you're not doing anything else, or staying on for the singing."

"*Nee,* I'm not staying. I'd like to go on a picnic with you."

"You would?"

When she nodded she could see in his face he was relieved. But who had wanted her there? Was it the girls who asked that she come, or was it Nathan?

She immediately thought about Marta and how she would feel about her going on a picnic with her recent ex-fiancé and his two daughters. She looked around and saw Marta talking to Adam. The two of them were engrossed in what the other had to say. They looked close, happy together. Deborah could see what was going on. Nathan had rejected Marta and now she realized she liked Adam better. At least, that's what Deborah hoped was happening.

"How about you come with us when the meeting is finished, and then I will bring you home later in the evening?" Nathan suggested.

"Okay. I'll let *Dat* know."

"I'll tell the girls. They'll be so pleased you're coming with us."

Deborah could not let herself be carried away thinking about a future with Nathan. If he had rejected Marta like Elizabeth said, why would he be interested in a plain overweight woman such as herself?

CHAPTER 22

Deborah

It surprised Deborah that Nathan already had a picnic basket prepared. Had he planned to go on a picnic with just the girls, or had he planned the picnic hoping she would go with them?

Nathan carried the picnic basket while the girls each held one of Deborah's hands.

Nathan said, "Emma, look for a nice grassy patch for us to put the blanket down on."

"Okay, *Dat*. This way, everyone."

Emma walked faster, still holding on to Deborah's hand.

"Don't go too fast, Emma. Grace can't keep up."

Emma slowed her pace. "Marta went on a picnic with us one time."

"Nee, she didn't," Grace said.

"She did so, a long time ago. You wouldn't remember."

Deborah wanted to change the subject so she could enjoy her time with Nathan without thinking of Marta.

"What about that nice grassy patch over there, Emma." She nodded her head to one side. "How does it look to you?"

Emma stared where Deborah had nodded and then yelled over her shoulder to her father. "Come on, *Dat.* We're leaving you behind."

He chuckled. "This picnic basket and blanket are heavy. You go on ahead and I'll catch up."

"Let's run," Emma said.

The two girls clutched harder on Deborah's hands and she didn't have any choice but to run along with them as their giggles filled the air.

"This will do, Emma," Deborah said when they reached the grassy patch. "What do you think?"

Emma stopped running and looked around the spot quite seriously. Then she nodded eagerly, and they waited until Nathan joined them. He placed everything down on the ground and then the girls helped spread out the blanket.

When they were all seated, Deborah asked, "What do you have in there?"

"The girls and I made quite a feast, didn't we?"

"Jah, and even Grace helped make the sandwiches."

"I put the butter on," Grace said, looking pleased with herself.

"Wait until you see how much food we

have, Miss Deborah." Emma lifted the lid of the basket.

Deborah peeked inside. "Oh, there is a lot of food."

"I told you." Emma giggled.

"We have chicken sandwiches and beef sandwiches," Nathan said, pointing at which was which.

"Very good. I was hoping you would use the leftovers for the weekend." Deborah had been raised not to waste food.

"What would you like first, Miss Deborah? Just say which one, you can have any."

"Yeah, just say which one," Grace said, not wanting to be left out of anything.

"I'd like to start with a chicken sandwich, please."

As Emma dove into the basket looking for a chicken sandwich, her father said, "Are you in charge of the food today, Emma?"

Emma giggled. *"Jah,* I am." She handed Deborah a sandwich and asked her father what he'd like.

Once they had eaten their fill of sandwiches, the girls wanted to play tag and Deborah was pleased to be left alone with Nathan.

"Where do they get their energy from?" he asked.

"They never seem to tire."

"I used to come to this place with Sally when Grace was just a *boppli.* She got sick after Grace was born and then rapidly went downhill. I guess you know that."

Deborah was surprised to hear him talk about his late wife because in all the time that she'd worked for him, he'd only mentioned her one or two times when she'd first started. "I don't remember much about her. I remember the two of you getting married and then Emma and then Grace being born."

He smiled. "She loved them so much. Each time they do something clever or say something funny, I want to tell her, but she's not here. I wonder if she sees them from her heavenly home."

“I’m sure she does. In some way, at least.” From his words, she sensed how lonely he was, but why hadn’t Marta filled that void for him? She wanted to know, but couldn’t ask him. "It must be hard raising the two of them without her."

"Thanks to people like you and Marta, it's been a lot easier."

"I'm glad to have been able to be of help."

"You are, more than you know."

Maybe he asked her on the picnic as a way of saying thank you for working for him.

He put his hand up to his mouth and cleared his throat. "If you don't mind me saying, I've noticed that you don't really go to many of the young people's gatherings. You never seem to stay on for the singings on Sunday evenings."

"I'm surprised you noticed."

His lips turned upward at the corners. "I asked about you."

"You did?"

He nodded.

"Who did you ask, and what did they say?"

"I asked a few people, and they each told me things which confirmed what I found to be true about you."

She frowned. "I hope that's a good thing."

"It is. You have a very quiet and calming nature, and you don't make a fuss about things. You just quietly go about doing what you have to do."

She looked down at the colored blanket examining all the different threads woven through it and not knowing how to respond. "I suppose I've always been very quiet. Or maybe I keep to myself."

"You're very mature for your age."

She looked up at him to see him smiling. "Do you think so?"

"I do."

"Maybe you think that because I'm quiet."

"What made you like that?" he asked.

"I suppose it's due to my size. People always stare at me. I always say I took after my father, and my sisters took after my mother. My friends say I'd be pretty if I lost weight." All of a sudden, she hiccupped. "Oh, excuse me." She put her fingertips up to her lips and giggled.

"To me, Deborah, you look just right."

"Really?"

He nodded.

She had hiccupped again. "Excuse me —again."

He laughed along with her.

“Come and play with us,” Emma called out to them.

“Shall we?” Deborah asked him.

“I will if you will,” Nathan said with a gleam in his eyes.

She stood up. “Let's do it.”

Together, they played tag with the girls. It was the most fun Deborah had had in quite some time.

CHAPTER 23

Marta
Months Later

"Haven't you made me wait long enough?" Adam asked.

Marta giggled. "I want to be sure."

"You said you wanted me to have a job, and now I've got one. I've saved as much money as I can."

"It's only been about six months."

"How long are you gonna make me wait, Marta?"

She looked around about her. It was a Sunday meeting and it felt like such a long time ago that she'd ceased work for Nathan. It was a relief to be away from being trapped in limbo not knowing where she stood. Looking back at Adam, she asked, "If we got married, where would we live?"

"Wherever you want to live."

She smiled at him. "It's not wherever I want to live, it's where it's possible for us to live. I don't really want to live with your *mudder.*"

"It wouldn't be so bad. Just say yes and I'll work things out."

To Marta's way of thinking, he'd had months to get things organized and figure it out. That was the man's job, so why hadn't he take the lead and made plans?

"We've got a lot of options. We could even rent a place. What does it matter as long as we're together?"

"I told you what matters to me."

"I know you struggled and your parents

struggled when you were younger, but that will never happen again. That's in your past, and you have to let it go."

"It's a fear and I'm not … I've tried to let it go, but it haunts me. When I have a family, I want everything to be perfect."

"We'll make it perfect, you and I, with *Gott's* help."

She looked into his deep brown eyes and nodded.

"What does that mean?"

She smiled and she knew it was right. "It means, let's do it."

"You mean it?"

"I do."

"I could kiss you right now." He looked around them. "But not here in front of the whole community. Let's leave."

She giggled. "Okay."

As Adam walked quickly to his buggy, Marta hurried to keep up with him. She knew going from one brother to the other had set some tongues wagging, but she didn't care. It was nobody's business. She finally knew that Adam was the man she wanted to spend her life with. He had worked hard the past six months and had stuck with a job that he didn't particularly like. Besides that, she knew he had a good heart and if he said that they'd make it work, then they would make it work.

ADAM'S MOTHER had stayed home from the meeting because she wasn't feeling well.

"I can't wait to tell *Mamm.* Come home now so we can tell her together."

They were still at the Sunday meeting, just about to leave. Marta continued to follow Adam toward the buggy. "Isn't she sick?"

"She's just feeling a little off. This news will make her feel much better."

Marta hoped so, but she wasn't too certain. Over two years ago, close to two and a half by now, Nathan and she had told her similar news—that she and Nathan were marrying.

Surely Adam's mother wouldn't be that surprised about the news; she had to expect it. Marta had been dating Adam for some time now. Marriage was the next logical progression. Now that more time had passed, Marta was pleased things hadn't worked out with Nathan.

"Do you think we should wait until she is feeling better?" Marta asked.

"This is news she's been waiting to hear."

When they walked into Adam's house, his mother was sitting down with a blanket covering her legs.

"*Mamm,* I have Marta with me."

She looked up. "Oh, Marta, come and sit down by me. Make us all some hot tea, would you, Adam?"

His mother started talking so much that now was not the right time to tell her the news. Adam headed into the kitchen while

Marta sat down next to her future mother-in-law.

"I was getting ready to go to the meeting today, and I might have been able to go in a couple more hours. The meeting starts so early that if I feel poorly in the morning there's no time to recover."

"Do you have a fever or something?"

"Sometimes I have trouble getting started in the morning. It's not a cold, a fever, or anything of that kind. If I'm achy when I wake up, I can't rush around to get ready."

"I hope you don't mind Adam bringing me here when you're not feeling well."

Adam walked back into the room.

Mrs. Beiler patted her hand. "Of course not. I like it when you visit. You brighten the place as much as a vase of flowers."

Marta giggled.

"Mamm, we have some news for you."

His mother stared at Adam and then glanced back at Marta. "What is it?"

"Marta has agreed to marry me."

She stared at Marta open mouthed. "This is good news. Does anyone else know?"

"You're the first."

She put a hand up to her mouth and gave a little giggle. Then a wistful look crossed her face. "It would be nice if your *vadder* could be here still, to see you boys married." She leaned forward and gave Marta a hug.

When she was finished hugging Marta, Adam stood up. "Do I get one?"

"Of course."

Adam leaned over and hugged his mother.

"It's so delightful that the two of you will be married and you'll give me more *grosskin.* When will you marry?"

"We haven't really discussed that yet," Marta said.

"We'll have to visit the bishop, and we'd like to set a date for as soon as possible." Adam glanced at Marta, and she smiled and nodded.

As soon as possible sounded good to her.

At last, she had someone who was looking forward to marriage as much as she. She'd waited a long time to make sure Adam was the right man for her and now she couldn't wait to get started on the next chapter of her life.

When the kettle whistled, Adam rose to his feet. Marta stood as well. "You stay here with your *mudder.* I'll get the tea."

Adam gave a nod and sat back down.

Marta headed to the kitchen pleased that Adam's mother was happy about their engagement. Everything was turning out well. There was no worrying about how Adam felt about her, nothing like there had been with Nathan. Her relationship with Adam had flowed nicely from beginning to end. If only she'd been brave enough to choose Adam years ago.

CHAPTER 24

Deborah

Deborah had just begun to walk home from Nathan's house on Monday evening, just on dusk, when she saw a familiar buggy coming toward her.

She stopped and waited. It was her family's buggy and her mother was driving while Jenny was in the back.

When it stopped close to her, she hurried over. "Where are you going?"

"I delayed my visit to Elizabeth today so you could come along," her mother told her.

"*Denke, Mamm*. That was thoughtful."

When she climbed in the buggy, Jenny handed her a sandwich. "I made you a sandwich because I thought you might be hungry and it will be a while before we come home and have dinner."

"That was very kind of you, Jenny. I'm grateful." Deborah opened the paper wrapper and bit right into the sandwich. Her sister had guessed right she was very hungry. If she didn't have a full-time job, Deborah thought as she ate, she would've spent most of her time helping Elizabeth with the new *boppli,* but her sister and mother seemed to have that covered.

WHEN THEIR MOTHER and Jenny were fussing over the baby, Deborah had time alone with Elizabeth in the living room.

"Marta came here today, and she told me that she's getting married."

Deborah froze as she sat on the couch, thinking she might be getting married to Nathan. "Who to?"

"Adam, of course."

Relief washed over Deborah. "Oh, that is good news."

"Don't tell me you've fallen for Nathan?"

Elizabeth knew her too well. "Is it that obvious?" Deborah asked.

"Just a smidgen."

"It's no use. If he didn't marry Marta he's not going to marry me."

"Why do you say that?" Elizabeth asked.

"Well, look at me." She spread out her hands and looked down at herself. "I'm just plain and dowdy. I'm nothing to look at."

"You're beautiful, Deborah."

Deborah laughed. "I know that I'm not. It doesn't bother me. I take after *Dat,* and you and Jenny take after *Mamm."*

"I don't know about that."

"It's true, I've got heavy bones and a heavy build, just like *Dat."* Deborah shrugged. "Anyway, that's just how it is. We get along all right, and I think he likes me as a friend or that kind of thing."

"Well, that's a good start. That's the best way—to be friends with someone before you start a relationship."

"I'm not even thinking like that because I don't want to get my hopes up."

Elizabeth smiled. "You should have your hopes up. You'll marry a lovely man, just you wait and see."

"I hope so, but if it doesn't happen, it doesn't happen. I'll just help you look after all your *bopplis."*

"Well, let's just start with one. I'm still getting used to Liz. Do you think that's a funny name for a *boppli?"*

"Nee, I think it's a beautiful name. And it suits her so well. She's the most beautiful baby I've ever seen."

"I think so too, and you'll think that about your own."

"Marta must be happy to be getting married at last."

"I don't know why things didn't work out with Nathan. They seem to be so well-suited."

"Maybe it was just too soon for him."

"That's what Marta said his excuse was. Anyway, I think she made the right decision. Adam really loves her."

DEBORAH WENT to work as usual the next day. When she walked in the door and saw Nathan, she knew something had changed between them. He looked at her differently, in a softer kind of way.

Could he like her?

She didn't dare to believe it could be true. For the first time, she allowed herself to think that marriage was a possibility.

If Nathan liked her even a little bit, that meant another man might actually love her. She wouldn't allow herself to consider a future with Nathan—that was something too good to be true.

At Marta and Adam's wedding three months later, something happened that gave Deborah some hope.

Everyone had gathered around the food tables outside Marta's house after the ceremony. Emma and Grace were with their grandmother, and Nathan walked up to Deborah just as she was about to sit down.

"Mind if I sit here, too?" he asked.

"That's fine." She sat and noticed he had no plate of food. "Aren't you eating?"

"I will later."

"It was a lovely wedding."

He nodded.

Deborah wondered whether he regretted

not marrying Marta when he had the chance. She leaned forward and almost whispered, "Does it feel funny that you nearly married Marta?"

He smiled. "A little, but she's a lovely girl. More suited to my *bruder.*"

Deborah nodded and took her first mouthful of food.

"There's someone I believe is more suited to me."

She looked into his deep brown eyes as she swallowed, hoping he'd say it was she. "Who's that?"

"Do you need to ask?"

Her heart pounded against her chest. *"Jah."*

"It's you, Deborah."

"Me?"

He chuckled. "I hope you feel the same, or now I'll feel stupid."

She stared at him, hardly able to breathe and lost for words. He was actually saying that he liked her. Well, more than liked her.

"Aren't you going to say anything?"

"I'm in shock."

Now he didn't reply and she knew she'd have to let him know she felt the same. "I do."

"You feel the same?"

She nodded.

His body relaxed. "Why don't I see if my *mudder* can take the girls for a night soon so we can go out for dinner, or do something together? Get to know one another better without the girls."

"I'd like that."

He chuckled softly. "I'll look forward to it. Now I can get some food, now that I've got that off my chest. I've been meaning to ask you for some time, but I was nervous about how you'd react. I thought you'd think me too old for you."

"You're not. Age doesn't matter. It's the person inside that counts."

He nodded. "You're right. That's exactly

what matters. I told you on that picnic how I feel about you."

"You don't mind the age difference?"

"You're mature, more mature than many women older than you. I like being around you." He couldn't say anything further as other people sat at the table. "I'll get my meal now."

Deborah was delighted that her weight wasn't mentioned in their conversation. She'd told him before how she felt about her size, and he didn't mind in the least.

She looked over at Marta and Adam and saw them laughing and talking to one another. It made her happy that Marta had found someone, just the right someone, after her disappointment with Nathan.

CHAPTER 25

Marta

It was the best day of Marta's life. She had the best man in the world for her. Adam had become the man she wanted, the man she had been waiting for. The pain of the long engagement to Nathan had been washed away. Nathan was now her brother-in-law and she held no resentment over the past.

They had to live with Adam's mother until they saved for a home of their own, and

Marta didn't mind. Mrs. Beiler was nice to her, and so happy to have her as a daughter-in-law. Then it hit her. Now she was Mrs. Beiler, too.

"I have a wedding surprise for you," Adam whispered.

"Another wedding gift?" she asked him.

"Not really."

"What is it?"

"You'll have to wait until I show you."

She playfully dug him in the ribs. *"Nee,* tell me now."

"Nee, I can't." When she pouted, he laughed. "Okay, but give me a smile first." When she smiled, he said, "We only have to live with my *Mamm* until our *haus* is built."

"We're building a *haus?"*

"Jah, and I was going to take you to the land and surprise you later today, but since I can't keep any secrets from you …"

"Oh, Adam, really?"

"Jah. I told you I'd never disappoint you. You'll never have to go without anything

ever again and neither will our *kinner.* We might have to cut a few corners, you might have to grow vegetables and we'll keep chickens."

"Of course, of course. I can do all that and more." Tears came to Marta's eyes. She felt like such a dreadful person. It shouldn't have mattered whether she was going to be poor or rich. God would always provide. She'd forced herself onto Nathan at a time when he was still recovering from his wife's death. And she'd plotted to put a plain woman in her place at Nathan's house. She silently prayed for God to forgive her wickedness.

"I hope I've done the right thing," he said.

She nodded. "You have. These are happy tears. *Denke.*"

She glanced over at Nathan and saw him talking closely with Deborah. He was looking at Deborah in a way that he'd never looked at her. Maybe it had been God's plan all along to have Deborah work for Nathan, and he'd used her in his plan to place Deborah in his house. If that was so, then all she'd been through had been worth it.

"What are you looking at?" Adam tried to follow the direction of her gaze.

"I'm looking at Nathan. He seems very interested in Deborah."

"Jah, he is. He told me so."

Marta opened her mouth wide. "Adam Beiler, now that I'm your *fraa* you must tell me everything."

He laughed. "It's not my secret to tell."

"All the same, you must tell me everything you know."

"I can't tell you other people's secrets."

"Why not? You just did."

Adam looked back at Nathan and Deborah as they sat eating on one end of a far table. "I only told you because it looks like it won't be a secret for much longer."

CHAPTER 26

Deborah

After the wedding, Deborah went home with Elizabeth so she could spend some time with her sister and her baby niece. Peter had stayed to help with the church benches that had to be loaded back onto the wagons, and to disassemble the food annexes.

When they got back to Elizabeth's house, they sat down in the living room. Baby Liz fell asleep in Deborah's arms.

"I'll put her in the crib," Elizabeth said.

"Nee, she's fine. I'll hold her. She's not heavy." Deborah placed a soft kiss on baby Liz's forehead.

"Okay."

She looked over at Elizabeth. "I found out today that Nathan likes me."

"You told me that."

"I told you I *thought* he did, but today I know for certain. He's going to get his *Mamm* to mind Emma and Grace so we can go on a proper date. What do you think about that?"

"I think it's *wunderbaar."*

"He doesn't mind that I'm fat."

"You're not really fat."

"I am, and I guess he's not that skinny either. It doesn't matter, though."

Elizabeth nodded. "I like him a lot. Look how good he was with Joshua. He had a good talk with him and Joshua's kept out of trouble ever since."

"He made him work off the money for

the bike. I like that he didn't let him off all together. He made Joshua see that there are consequences for his actions," Deborah said. "He'll be a *gut vadder* for a boy if ..."

"If you and Nathan have one?"

Deborah giggled.

Elizabeth nodded. "It's true. Joshua was heading down a dark path."

"He was, and it shows how good Nathan is with *kinner.*"

"Yeah, if you have a boy like Joshua, he'll know exactly what to do."

They both giggled.

"How good was it that Marta chose you to be the temporary nanny when she went away?"

"Jah. It was, or I never would've gotten close to him."

"See how *Gott* has worked everything out? Adam and Marta are now married and you and Nathan might be next."

"Oh, Elizabeth, do you think it might

come to that? Do you think we might marry?"

"Jah, I do. It'd be a good match. He's perfect for you and you'll have a ready-made *familye."*

"I love Emma and Grace. I always wanted lots of *kinner,* but I never thought it'd happen. I don't want to get my hopes up, but that's all I can think about."

"Just pray about it and it'll happen, if he's the right man for you."

"I know, you're right. That's what I'll do. Do you think he'll ask me to marry him?"

Elizabeth nodded. "It sounds like he might. What will you say if he does?"

"I'll marry him if he asks me." She thought back to how she'd had the childhood crush on him. In her daydreams, she'd imagined being married to him, and then he'd married Sally. That had been the end of it, she'd thought.

CHAPTER 27

It was Wednesday night when Nathan arranged for his mother to look after the girls. Nathan collected Deborah at her home, the girls with him in the buggy, and then the plan was to take the girls to his mother's while Nathan and Deborah had dinner somewhere.

Deborah climbed into the buggy and before she had a chance to say hello, the girls asked her if she'd marry their father.

Deborah didn't know what to say.

"Can you, Miss Deborah?" Grace asked.

"Jah, because Marta can't marry *Dat* anymore because she's married to *Onkel* Adam."

"Now she's Aunt Marta, so she can't be our *mudder,"* Grace said.

"Girls! It's impolite to say things like that," their father said.

"Why?" Grace asked.

"It just is," Nathan answered.

"But why?" Grace persisted.

"He'll never say why," Emma told her younger sister.

"Unfair."

Deborah exchanged smiles with Nathan. When they arrived at his mother's house, Deborah sat in the buggy and waited for the girls to be taken inside.

"I'm sorry about that," he said when he climbed back in.

"Don't be."

"They have the right idea, though."

She smiled at him and he moved his

horse forward. Now she knew he had marriage on his mind. Before they got to the restaurant, Nathan moved his horse and buggy off the road.

In a daze Deborah asked, "Are we here?"

He chuckled. *"Nee,* there's nothing but fields and trees surrounding us."

"Oh. Sorry, I was lost in my thoughts."

"I had everything planned out in my head. A romantic dinner, for just the two of us. Then I was going to steer the conversation around to you and me." He sighed. "I can't wait a moment longer." He shifted in his seat to face her more fully. "Deborah, these days with you have been the happiest I've known in years. Since you started work at my *haus,* I've felt like I can breathe again. I want you in my life forever."

She gulped when she realized what he was saying.

"Deborah, would you consider marrying me?"

Her fingertips went to her mouth and she covered her smile. As she did so, some hair made its way out of her prayer *kapp* and covered her face. Gently with his fingertips, he pushed the hair away from her face.

"You don't have to give me an answer now," he almost whispered.

She didn't want to miss the opportunity. "I can answer you now." She looked directly into his dark brown eyes.

"Well, what do you say?"

"Jah, I will marry you."

"You will?" She nodded and he took hold of her hand. "I never thought I'd find happiness again. Are you sure?"

"I am. I'm very sure."

His face lit up. "What shall we do? I want to tell everyone. Or should we continue on to dinner and plan the rest of our lives together?"

She nodded. *"Jah,* let's have our dinner. That will give me time to get used to it."

He leaned forward and kissed her on her cheek, setting off what felt like a million tingles through her body. When she opened her eyes, the buggy was moving. It felt like she was dreaming.

Over dinner, he suggested a date for their wedding. When he did so, she agreed with the date and breathed a sigh of relief. She wasn't going to have the same experience as Marta where a date was never set. After that, she could barely eat and was scarcely able to concentrate on anything else he said.

THEY AGREED to wait until they got the bishop's approval on the date for the wedding before they told the rest of their families, including Emma and Grace.

Marta and Adam had found out at the same time, when Deborah had been invited to a family dinner at Adam and Nathan's mother's house. Everyone was delighted to hear the news, and Marta was especially pleased. When the adults were congratulating them, Nathan's girls were bubbling with enthusiasm.

"We're going to have a *mudder?*" Emma asked.

"Jah, that's right," Nathan said. "Miss Deborah will be your *mudder."*

"And mine too?" Grace asked.

"That's right," Deborah told her. Deborah knew that everything had worked out how it was meant. Marta was genuinely happy for them, she could see it in her eyes.

"We'll be *schweschders*-in-law, Deborah," Marta said.

"That's right. I'm so glad!" The unfriendliness that Deborah had felt from Marta in the past was now gone. Marriage to Adam had softened her and made her content.

Directly after that family dinner, Nathan, Deborah and the girls went to tell the good news to Deborah's family.

Her family were all just as pleased. After

desserts and tea at the Fishers' house, it was time for Nathan and the girls to head home. Deborah walked them back out to their buggy. The girls kept yawning, but kept insisting they didn't want to go to bed.

"This was a big day, wasn't it?" Deborah said to Nathan.

"It was, and a very happy one too."

She glanced at the girls in the back of the buggy and then whispered to Nathan, *"Denke* for making me so happy." She gazed into his eyes and silently thanked God for creating Nathan and for bringing them together.

"Nee, it's me who needs to thank you. Every morning when I count my blessings, you're now at the top of that list."

Deborah could scarcely contain her joy. Her daydreams had turned into reality and even better, she had Emma and Grace, two sweet girls, and she would start her married life with a ready-made family.

Thank you for reading The Temporary Amish Nanny.

For a downloadable series reading order of all Samantha Price's books, scan below or head to: SamanthaPriceAuthor.com

THE NEXT BOOK IN THE SERIES

Book 6:
Jeremiah's Daughter

Beverly vowed never to return after she left the Amish community after a huge row with her step mother. Ten years on, she has little choice but to return after a frantic call from her father. Their bed-and-breakfast was failing and with Beverly's background in finance, her father was convinced she was the only one who could turn things around.

AMISH MISFITS

Book 7 My Brother's Keeper

ABOUT SAMANTHA PRICE

Samantha Price is a USA Today bestselling author of Amish romance books and cozy mysteries. She was raised Brethren and has a deep affinity for the Amish way of life, which she has explored extensively with over a decade of research.

She is mother to two pampered rescue cats, and a very spoiled staffy with separation issues.

www.SamanthaPriceAuthor.com

Made in the USA
Monee, IL
23 November 2024

71010672R10136